MONSTERS

A DARK DRABBLES ANTHOLOGY

Compiled & Edited by D Kershaw

Also available from Black Hare Press

DARK DRABBLES ANTHOLOGIES

WORLDS
ANGELS
BEYOND
UNRAVEL

Twitter: @BlackHarePress
Facebook: BlackHarePress
Website: www.BlackHarePress.com

A catalogue record for this book is available from the National Library of Australia

ISBN 978-1-925809-18-3

Cover Design by Dawn Burdett
Book Formatting by Ben Thomas

The last glimpse I had was of the bloated face,

blood-stained and fixed with a grin of malice

which would have held its

own in the nethermost hell.

- Bram Stoker, "Dracula"

Table of Contents

Foreword

We all love monsters.

From the youngest age, we're fascinated by the fiendish and furry, the creepiest critters, the naughty and the nasty. So, it's unsurprising that so many authors wanted to contribute to this book of tiny terrors.

And they didn't disappoint!

But be warned; you're going to learn that monsters are *everywhere*. They're under your bed, in the closet, down in the cellar, in the mirror…in your *head*. The likes of which you didn't know existed.

So, close the drapes, check the locks, turn on all the lights, and get comfortable.

But don't close your eyes…because they're waiting…

Love and kisses
D. Kershaw & Ben Thomas
Black Hare Press

Zombie Sonnet 43
by Henry Herz

How do I eat thee? Let me count the ways.

I love thee to the depth and breadth

My slavering jaws can reach and my teeth tear.

For your frontal lobes and bone's marrow,

I'll gnaw under sickly moonlight

To the end of every night's most ravenous need.

I eat thee freely, as a spider feasts on bound prey.

I devour thee purely, as a vampire a virgin's blood.

I gorge on thee with a damned hunger for organ meat.

I befoul thee with pestilent corpse breath.

Now that I've risen from the grave,

I love thee better after death.

Henry Herz edited the dark fantasy anthology, BEYOND THE PALE, featuring stories by Saladin Ahmed, Peter Beagle, Heather Brewer, Jim Butcher, Rachel Caine, Kami Garcia, Nancy Holder, and Jane Yolen. His horror story, Gluttony, will appear in the anthology, CLASSICS REMIXED. He authored the children's books: MONSTER GOOSE NURSERY RHYMES, WHEN YOU GIVE AN IMP A PENNY, MABEL & THE QUEEN OF DREAMS, LITTLE RED CUTTLEFISH, CAP'N REX & HIS CLEVER CREW, HOW THE SQUID GOT TWO LONG ARMS, ALICE'S MAGIC GARDEN, GOOD EGG AND BAD APPLE, TWO PIRATES + ONE ROBOT, THE MAGIC SPATULA, and I AM SMOKE.
Website: www.henryherz.com

Kismet
by Umair Mirxa

Katrina lounged across the couch, watching the three couples waltz around the room, and licked the blood off her fangs. She imagined all the ways she could kill them. Rip them apart. None excited her. Not how they had in the past.

A 300-year-old vampire, she had graciously dealt with everything that kismet had thrown at her over the centuries. Her transition, the constant hunger, the urge to kill. A dozen lifetimes of men and women fawning over her. She had done all there was to do, and more.

Now, she was bored. Slowly, she drained her six victims dry.

Umair Mirxa lives in Karachi, Pakistan. His first published story, 'Awareness', appeared on Spillwords Press. He has also had stories accepted for anthologies from Zombie Pirate Publishing, Blood Song Books, Fantasia Divinity Magazine and Publishing, and Iron Faerie Publishing. He is a massive J.R.R. Tolkien fan, and loves everything to do with fantasy and mythology. He enjoys football, history, music, movies, TV shows, and comic books, and wishes with all his heart that dragons were real.
Website: www.umairmirxa.com
Facebook: UMirxa12

Food Chain
by Joshua D. Taylor

The werewolf didn't feel bad about eating the jogger. It was the natural way of things, he thought, as he devoured his victim on a forest trail. Cows eat grass. People eat cows. Werewolves eat people.

Several long muscular tentacles slipped from the canopy above him. They wrapped around him and pulled him off the ground. Before he could let out a howl, a razor-sharp beak bit through his neck, nearly decapitating him. The tree squid didn't feel bad about eating the werewolf. It was the natural way of things. People eat cows. Werewolves eat people. Tree squid eat werewolves.

Joshua D. Taylor is an amateur writer who started writing a few years ago when he realised he was too old to play make-believe. He lives in southeastern Pennsylvania with his wife and a one-eared cat. He enjoys gardening, comic books, ska-punk music, Disney World, and travelling with his wife. Raised during weirdness that was the late 20th century Josh's eclectic interests produce eclectic works. He loves to mix-n-match things from different genres and stories elements to achieve a madcap hodgepodge of the truly unexpected. His short story 'the Obelisk' appears in Salty Tales by Stormy Island Publishing.
Facebook: authorjoshuadtaylor

Haute Cuisine
by Carole de Monclin

"No, no, no… We won't make burgers. Grinding this meat would be a sacrilege. You let it age, grow into its flavour."

"Fine by me. I hunted, you cook. Just make sure it isn't dry."

"A marinade maybe? Not too much, though. I don't want to overpower the meat's character."

"Béarnaise sauce, rather?"

"You got it. Where did you find game this good?"

"Wandering into a dark alley. It got separated from the pack."

"Think all the alcohol will give it a weird taste?"

"Nah. Just a little kick."

Hunched over the lifeless woman, both ghouls licked their chops in anticipation.

Carole de Monclin has lived in France and Australia, but for the moment the USA is home. She finds inspiration from her travels. She loves Science Fiction because it explores the human mind in a way no other genre can. Plus, who doesn't love spaceships and lasers? Her stories appear in the Exoplanet Magazine and Angels - A Dark Drabbles Anthology.
Website: CaroledeMonclin.com
Twitter: @CaroledeMonclin

Daddy Long Legs
by J. Farrington

"Moooooooom! There's a spider in my room!" Nat yelled downstairs from her bedroom doorway.

Not slowing from washing dishes, her mother replied, "Throw it out then!"

"I don't think I can it's…just come look please. It's a Daddy Long Legs!" A waiver in her voice put the hairs on her mother's arm on edge. Stepping away from the sink, she headed upstairs.

"Look!" Nat pointed into the room. Leaning into the room her mother came face to face with a socks and sandal wearing 10ft spider.

"What in the— Ok I'm confused" she muttered under her breath.

"Hi confused…I'm Dad"

J. Farrington is an aspiring author from the West Midlands, UK. His genre of choice is horror; whether that be psychological, suspense, supernatural or straight up weird, he'll give it a shot! He has loved writing from a young age but has only publicly been spreading his darker thoughts and sinister imagination via social platforms since 2018. If you would like to view his previous work, or merely lurk in the shadows...watching, you can keep up to date with future projects by spirit board or alternatively, the following;
Twitter: @SurvivorTrench
Reddit: TrenchChronicles

Snotmen
by Brian Rosenberger

"Any change?" questioned the Chief

"No, Sir," answered Deputy Brooks. "No change in the witness."

"Keep me posted."

"Yes, Sir."

Chief DelGado settled behind his desk and reviewed the case. Male teenager. Sole witness to his parents' double homicide. The crime scene photos—the images hardly recognisable as human.

When questioned, the boy had the same emotionless response.

"Snotmen."

Over and over.

Outside. Gunfire. Multiple shots.

Deputy Brooks shouted, "Come quick."

The Chief peeked between blinds, witnessed Hell walking the streets.

Thoughts of his two boys, his wife.

"Not men," Chief Delgado echoed and pointed his revolver at his temple.

Brian Rosenberger lives in a cellar in Marietta, GA (USA) and writes by the light of captured fireflies. He is the author of As the Worms Turns and three poetry collections. He is also a featured contributor to the Pro-Wrestling literary collection, Three-Way Dance, available from Gimmick Press.
Facebook: HeWhoSuffers

Beauty and the Beastly Revelation
by John H. Dromey

Midnight. Time for unmasking. Olivia was anxious to behold the everyday appearance of the stranger with whom she'd danced the night away. She fancied herself the belle of the ball and Hugh had matched her step for step.

She held her breath as her partner peeled off his mask.

The young man's face was covered with garish red welts and streaks. If possible, his visage was even more horrific than that of the pretend monster he'd portrayed earlier.

Olivia screamed, then fled in terror.

Hugh called out to her. 'Come back! The condition is only temporary. I'm allergic to latex!"

John H. Dromey was born in northeast Missouri, USA. He enjoys reading—mysteries in particular—and writing in a variety of genres. He's had short fiction published in Alfred Hitchcock's Mystery Magazine, Martian Magazine, Stupefying Stories Showcase, Thriller Magazine, Unfit Magazine, and elsewhere, as well as in a number of anthologies, including Chilling Horror Short Stories (Flame Tree Publishing, 2015).

The Hunter
by Eddie D. Moore

A breeze rattled the upper branches of the trees, and the deer Eric was watching through his scope froze. The underbrush blocked his shot, and he waited patiently for the deer to take one more step. He blinked when something large pounced on top of the deer.

Fur flew and blood sprayed onto the trees. The struggle was over in seconds, and when the creature stopped to feed, Eric saw its red eyes and razor-sharp teeth. It tore away mouthfuls of meat with each shake of its head. In awe, Eric whispered, "Gargoyle."

The gargoyle growled and glared at Eric.

Eddie D. Moore travels hundreds of hours a year, and he fills that time by listening to audiobooks. When he isn't playing with his grandchildren, he writes his own stories. You can find a list of his publications on his blog or by visiting his Amazon Author Page. While you're there, be sure to pick up a copy of his mini-anthology Misfits & Oddities.
Website: eddiedmoore.wordpress.com
Amazon: amazon.com/author/eddiedmoore

Collector of Souls
by J.D. Bell

"It is not so difficult to steal the essence of a man," the stranger said to his dinner companion. "They say the eyes are the window to the soul." He looked deep into the man's eyes. "I'll show you."

The stranger locked the man's gaze on his. As much as he tried, the man could not look away. His eyes began to bleed, and his skull felt as if it would burst from within. Images from his life faded from his mind. The stranger released his grip, satisfied that he had drained every ounce of the man's being into himself.

J.D. Bell is an award-winning, internationally published, author of flash fiction and short stories. He recently retired from the world of writing advertising copy and is now enjoying the universe of creative fiction.
Facebook: jim.writes.stories
Twitter: @JimBell58

Camp North
by Denny E. Marshall

Matt jumps off the train as it slows. Matt rode the rails further north than usual hoping to escape the heat wave covering most of the country. He looks for a hobo camp.

It took Matt time to find one since this is his first visit to the area. As he walks into the camp, he has a strange feeling, but shrugs it off. Matt is a muscular guy.

After a brief rest inside the camp, a group of twenty surrounds him. Matt is overwhelmed with fear.

Matt didn't realise until that moment there are hobo camps for poor vampires.

Denny E. Marshall has had art, poetry, and fiction published. One recent credit is fiction in Night To Dawn 35 April 2019.
Website: www.dennymarshall.com

Stupid Monsters
by Jensen Reed

"They're stupid, emotionless bags of crap, Hannah," Marco teased. He turned to make faces at the zombies on the other side of the chain-link, and I tensed.

"Please," I whined, "I just want to go."

Marco rolled his eyes and stepped away from the fence. The metal groaned against the weight of pushing bodies as we continued to school. I tried to fight the eerie feeling in my stomach but failed. I looked over my shoulder and froze at the blood splattered zombie on this side of the fence. A scream stuck in my throat when it smiled at me.

Jensen Reed is a multi-published short story author, lead admin for Writing Bad, and mama to two boys. She dabbles in reading and writing genres but particularly enjoys feeding characters to zombies and making readers cry. Find her book links, flash fiction, and connect with her on her website. Website: authorjensenreed.wordpress.com

Monster Buck
by Derek Dunn

The grass is too tall. We can't see its head, but the antlers rise over the back of its shoulders. It looks like a twelve pointer.

We stay squatted, holding our position. Bruce raises his rifle and takes aim. This is his buck. He's been watching it for weeks, only getting glimpses before it sprints away, never showing its face.

Bruce rises, but something snaps.

The buck turns. Bruce drops. The creature lunges toward us. A huge gaping mouth covers the entirety of its face. Hundreds of sharp fangs protrude from a bottomless pit.

It takes Bruce in one gulp.

Derek Dunn lives in the American Northwest with his family. He's a film enthusiast and musician who writes primarily horror and mystery stories.
Twitter: @DerekTDunn

Debt
by Andrew Anderson

"Good evening, sir. You'll recall that you recently sold your soul to the devil?"

"Um, yeah. Who…"

"Turns out Old Nick is a lousy card player. He got in way over his head the other night. I've bought your debt, and I'm here to collect."

"Huh, so…"

"Well, I'm afraid the original fee has gone up; the price is two souls now. Real estate in the Otherworld is pretty expensive these days."

"What, that's ridic—"

"I don't make the rules, and a demon like me has many mouths to feed. Come on, I haven't got all millennia; name the soul…"

Andrew Anderson is a full-time civil servant, dabbling in writing music, poetry, screenplays and short stories in his limited spare time, when not working on building himself a fort made out of second-hand books. He lives in Bathgate, Scotland with his wife, two children and his dog.
Twitter: @soorploom

Harlequin
by Zoey Xolton

Tiarna sobbed, tears streaking her white face paint. Her red eyes watched her reflection in despair. It grinned back at her with a deep, unsettling malice. She picked up a tissue and roughly wiped at her face again, smudging her comical mask.

Dropping the tissue, she picked up a smaller mirror from her vanity. She screamed, the mirror shattering on the floor. Her clown face was still there. Perfectly creepy once more, as if she'd never tried to remove it.

She raised her eyes to the large vanity mirror with its garish light bulbs. Her reflection smirked.

"Smile!" it taunted.

Zoey Xolton is an Australian Speculative Fiction writer, primarily of Dark Fantasy, Paranormal Romance and Horror. She is also a proud mother of two and is married to her soul mate. Outside of her family, writing is her greatest passion. She is especially fond of short fiction and is working on releasing her own themed collections in future. Website: www.zoeyxolton.com

Black Widow
by Dawn DeBraal

Stan and Doris were married in Las Vegas, Doris' fifth marriage. Doris was called the Black Widow because all of her husbands died; the marriage lasted about as long as the honeymoon did.

Stan told Doris they needed to reign in the spending as he carried her over the threshold. The next morning, Doris gave Stan his morning coffee.

"This coffee is wonderful. What's in it?" Stan asked.

"Almond extract." Doris Smiled.

Stan put his hands to his throat in the universal sign of choking as he fell to the floor. Doris kicked the cell phone out of his hand.

Dawn DeBraal lives in rural Wisconsin with her husband, two rat terriers, and a cat. She successfully raised two children (meaning they didn't return to the nest!) After many years serving the government at the Federal and County level, she recently retired. Having extra time on her hands she started to write after a paralyzed vocal cord took her ability to speak for two months. Not finding her voice, she discovered that her love of telling a good story could be written. Her works have been published in Palm-sized press, Spillwords, Mercurial Stories, Potato Soup Journal, and Blood Song Books.

Night Howl
by A.R. Johnston

She looked up to the gorgeous shine of the moon above her. It was a beautiful summer night, warm, and clear. The moon and stars shone bright, reflecting off the lake in front of her. The first tingles of magic spread across her skin and she shivered.

She didn't try to fight it or suppress it. She wanted this, and her inner beast was joyous in anticipation of a hunt. She dropped to her knees groaning, bones cracking, reshaping, fur flowing over her body. She lifted her muzzle and let loose a howl that echoed back. The night was hers.

A.R. Johnston is a small-town girl from Nova Scotia, Canada. Her style of writing is considered Urban Fantasy. Her first major publication is part of an anthology called First Love and she has several more titles lined up. She is a lover of coffee, good tv shows, horror flicks, and reader of books. She pretends to be a writer when real life doesn't get in the way. Pesky full-time job and adulting!

A Chance Encounter
by G. Allen Wilbanks

"Well, hello there, little guy. What are you?"

Mitchell knelt on the forest path to get a closer look at the white furred creature. No larger than his fist, and with no visible extremities, he would never have known it was alive except for two, large blue eyes peering up at him.

A tiny mouth appeared below the eyes. "Eeep!" it cried.

"That's adorable," Mitchell laughed, poking a finger at the tiny creature.

Needle-sharp teeth nipped his finger, drawing blood. Mitchell had no time to run as a thousand more small balls of white fur dropped from the trees above.

G. Allen Wilbanks is a member of the Horror Writers Association (HWA) and has published over 50 short stories in various magazines and on-line venues. He is the author of two short story collections, and the novel, When Darkness Comes.
Website: www.gallenwilbanks.com
Blog: DeepDarkThoughts.com

The Attic
by Greg Fewer

There it was again: a strange scrabbling above the ceiling! Rats? On my first night in the manor house which my uncle left me, I was trying to sleep in the guest room.

Leaving my bed, flashlight in hand, I went out onto the poorly lit landing and climbed up the ladder propped against the wall beneath the attic trapdoor. Reaching it, I pushed the trapdoor upwards and broke through a mass of cobwebs.

Something big and hard dropped onto me, stabbing my shoulder. Stiffening as I fell, I saw its eight red eyes follow me downwards.

Not rats then...

Greg Fewer has had genre flash fiction published in Cuento Magazine, Page & Spine: Fiction Showcase, The Sirens Call and Trembling With Fear.

The Monster Within
By Olivia Arieti

Gordon was familiar with evil; depraved and mischievous, no criminal or crime had been wicked enough for him until that night. No sooner had he gone to bed, than he sensed a deep pain as though his body was being torn apart. A few seconds after, the most hideous monster with drooping jaws and demoniac eyes stood before him.

Seized by terror, he snatched his knife and plunged it straight into the beast's heart just as the horrifying creature jumped back inside him.

A loud, inhuman cry resounded in the room; Gordon had killed the monster within his own self.

Olivia Arieti has a degree from the University of Pisa and lives in Torre del Lago Puccini, Italy, with her family. Besides being a published playwright, she loves writing retellings of fairy tales, and at the same time is intrigued by supernatural and horror themes. Her stories appeared in several magazines and anthologies like Enchanted Conversations, Enchanted Tales Literary Magazine, Fantasia Divinity Magazine, Cliterature, Medieval Nightmares, Static Movement, 100 Doors To Madness Forgotten Tomb Press, Black Cats Horrified Press, Bloody Ghost Stories Full Moon Books, Death And Decorations Thirteen O'Clock Press, Infective Ink, Pandemonium Press, Pussy Magic Magazine.

The Wendigo
by Michael Crow

Bob was a gluttonous slob. Locals talked of the Wendigo, the avatar of sensualists. Thin grey, leathery skin draped over bones like laundry over a clothesline. His face sunken in like a long-dead corpse. Bob's life of excess, now an eternity of hunger, a punishment for wrongs committed.

The Wendigo lurched forward toward the unsuspecting man sleeping beside the fire. The man awoke startled, but it was too late. The Wendigo seized the terrified man by the face and sucked the life from him. The Wendigo dropped the grey, lifeless corpse and trudged toward the light of the nearby town.

Michael Crow spends his sparse free time writing about sports, as well as working on his own fiction. Michael is the owner of Real Dead Review, a blog devoted to dark fiction. Michael's non-fiction works have appeared on USA Today, Fansided Network, The Guillotine, and Intermat. Michael makes his home with his wife, daughter and two cats in Central Minnesota.

Windigo
by Alanna Robertson-Webb

The thing stalking my campsite is a creature known as a Windigo, or something like it.

At first, I thought that it was just a buck, until I looked at it through the scope of my rifle. Its head is mostly bone, with ragged bits of decomposing flesh hanging off of it.

As I stared at it, the thing looked right at me, and a shiver jolted down my spine. I ran like a scared child, and I've been cowering in my tent for the last hour as it prowls around. I need to find a way out of here.

Alanna Robertson-Webb is a sales support member by day, and a writer and editor by night. She loves VT, and lives in NY. She has been writing since she was five years old, and writing well since she was seventeen years old. She lives with a fiance and a cat, both of whom take up most of her bed space. She loves to L.A.R.P., and one day she aspired to write a horrifyingly fantastic novel. Her short horror stories have been published before, but she still enjoys remaining mysterious.
Reddit: MythologyLovesHorror

The Magnificent Unicorn
by Crystal L. Kirkham

"Hurry," Carl said as they watched the magnificent unicorn grazing in the field. They needed proof before their portal to this realm closed.

Not wanting to startle it, Anne walked cautiously into the field. It looked up and she froze. When it didn't run she continued, hand outstretched towards it, and the unicorn lowered its head

Unexpectedly, it lunged forward, impaling her with its horn. She crumpled to the ground and it struck at her with golden hooves until she stilled.

Horrified, Carl watched it tear into her flesh and he understood why unicorns had been banished by the ancients.

Crystal L. Kirkham resides in a small hamlet west of Red Deer, Alberta. She's an avid outdoors person, unrepentant coffee addict, part-time foodie, servant to a wonderful feline, and companion to two delightfully hilarious canines. She will neither confirm nor deny the rumours regarding the heart in a jar on her desk and the bottle of reader's tears right next to it. Her paranormal urban fantasy series, Saints and Sinners, is available on Amazon and her YA Fantasy, Feathers and Fae will be released October 11, 2019, from Kyanite Publishing.
Website: www.crystallkirkham.com

Red Blood Cheddar
by Beth W. Patterson

"What is it about Americans and their orange cheese?" people ask me.

Well, I'll tell you. Cursed are the cheese makers. So driven are my entrepreneurial countrymen, they sacrifice their life-sustaining fluids to those bloodsucking dairy products until a hint of colour is absorbed. Thirsty and amorphous, the addiction is mutual.

On my last trip overseas, that nice old man in Oodnadatta heard my accent and good-naturedly asked me if I had a gun in my bag. The cheese hiding in there whispered, "Prove him wrong, and tonight I'll be eating crow."

And this is why the cheese stands alone.

Beth W. Patterson was a full-time musician for over two decades before diving into the world of writing, a process she describes as "fleeing the circus to join the zoo". She is the author of the books Mongrels and Misfits, and The Wild Harmonic, and a contributing writer to twenty anthologies. Patterson has performed in eighteen countries, expanding her perspective as she goes. Her playing appears on over a hundred and sixty albums, soundtracks, videos, commercials, and voice-overs (including seven solo albums of her own). She lives in New Orleans, Louisiana with her husband Josh Paxton, jazz pianist extraordinaire.
Website: www.bethpattersonmusic.com
Facebook: bethodist

Waiting for Dawn
by Joel R. Hunt

Light keeps them at bay. That's what the village priest told her. Now, as she watched its smoke-like essence bleeding through the keyhole, she prayed he was right.

As it reached the floor, the black mist condensed into a cruel hound, eyes glowing like coals, paws burning the bare wooden floor. Back and forth it prowled, testing the edge of the flickering lamplight, waiting for its chance. A second of darkness would be enough.

She shivered. The sunlight of morning would save her, but her lamp didn't have enough oil to last until dawn. She knew that.

Did the hound?

Joel R. Hunt *is a writer from the UK who dabbles in the darker aspects of life, particularly through horror, science fiction and the supernatural. He has been published here and there (though likely nowhere you've heard of) and hopes to have released his first anthology of short stories later this year.*
Twitter: @JoelRHunt1
Reddit: JRHEvilInc

Horace
by Rich Rurshell

When your grandad names a spider Horace, you know it's going to be big.

I thought he'd lost it when he brought in the steak and rang the bell on the fireplace.

"Horace! Dinner!"

After a sickening scuttling and scratching sound, Horace appeared.

It was huge! So big, I could look it in the face…and it looked back at me! Grandad dropped the steak and it turned its attention from me, grabbing the meat in its jaws and disappearing back up the chimney.

A dog collar fell down.

"Max didn't run away did he, Grandad."

"No…but he tried."

Rich Rurshell is a short story writer from Suffolk, England. Rich writes Horror, Sci-Fi, and Fantasy, and his stories can be found in various short story anthologies and magazines. Most recently, his story "Subject: Galilee" was published in World War Four from Zombie Pirate Publishing, and "Life Choices" was published in Salty Tales from Stormy Island Publishing. When Rich is not writing stories, he likes to write and perform music.
Facebook: richrurshellauthor

Feeding Time
by G. Allen Wilbanks

"It's horrible," said the woman, standing at the edge of the pond.

Beneath the water, a creature, vaguely humanoid in form, stared back with large yellow eyes. Its mouth gaped wide, revealing dozens of pointed, dagger-sharp teeth.

"Why would you own such a thing?"

The man behind her shrugged. "Many people collect exotic animals. I was fortunate enough to discover and capture it, so I kept it."

"Is it dangerous?"

"Not really. It can't leave the water."

"What do you feed it?" she asked.

The man moved closer. She felt his breath on her ear. "Funny you should ask that."

G. Allen Wilbanks is a member of the Horror Writers Association (HWA) and has published over 50 short stories in various magazines and on-line venues. He is the author of two short story collections, and the novel, When Darkness Comes.
Website: www.gallenwilbanks.com
Blog: DeepDarkThoughts.com

Buried Alive
by John Saxton

Stifling. Dark. Sticky… Tethered to the wall by my midriff.

What's that? An incessant drumming. Stretching out my arms, feeling blindly, touching claustrophobic prison walls. Soft, padded—*wet… What are they planning for me?*

Unease and confusion quickly become terror and despair. *Are they going to drown me, here in the dark?*

Have to escape. I flex my fingers—razor-sharp talons emerge from the tips. Wicked-needle fangs unsheathe from riven gums.

The fabric of the prison yields to my ripping, slicing claws.

The midwife screams as the demon emerges, snarling from the ragged flesh—and the host-mother's booming heart stops.

John Saxton hails from Yorkshire, UK, where he is happily married, with two sons. He has had over 50 short horror stories published in the independent press, including his own collection: 'Bloodshot'. He writes mainly after dark...
Twitter: @jsaxtonwriter

Something Inside
by Terry Miller

Eyelids sealed shut, something squirming in my ears, and the smell of death climbing up my nostrils isn't exactly the way I wanted to wake up. I felt a stick in my arm and seconds later I was calm again. The gnawing at the tips of my fingers made me uneasy, the sensation of tiny legs scurrying from atop my arm tickled the epidermis.

I drifted in and out of consciousness, voices reduced to inaudible mumbles as the things in my ears burrowed deeper. No, not mumbles. Not voices. Not human. No, something else, something inside; tunnelling. Something hungry, feeding.

Terry Miller is an author and 2017 Rhysling Award-nominated poet residing in Portsmouth, OH, USA. He has self-published a dark poetry collection on Amazon and one short story to date. His work has also appeared in Sanitarium, Devolution Z, Jitter Press, Poetry Quarterly, O Unholy Night in Deathlehem, and the 2017 Rhysling Anthology from the Science Fiction and Fantasy Poetry Association.
Facebook: tmiller2015

Maid and Monster
by S. Gepp

Thorvald reined his horse.

He dismounted and approached with caution.

The bloodied woman's eyes flickered. She couldn't speak. Her eyes darted left.

Thorvald swung his sword from his back.

The beast crashed through the trees. Its claws glistened with fresh red. Its angry roar echoed off every surface.

Thorvald's horse reared and bolted.

Thorvald, though, stood his ground.

It charged him. At the last moment, Thorvald ducked and then jumped and thrust his sword.

The creature screeched, blood pumping from its pierced eye, then fled.

Thorvald lifted the woman.

"Thankyou," she whispered adoringly.

He smiled. A good day, he decided.

S. Gepp is an Australian, with two children, two university degrees (and counting), two tertiary education diplomas, and a resumé that looks like a list of every job you could ever have without really trying, including stints as a school teacher, scientist, editor and journalist. He has also been a performance acrobat, a professional wrestler, a stand-up comedian and an actor. He has been writing for 30 years (with some publications: one novella, about 10 poems, 40-odd short stories, and a few more pending) and hopes to be a real writer if he grows up. A dull life.

The Ice Cream Man
by Dawn DeBraal

The ice cream truck's music sped up as Lenard stepped on the gas. The little kids wanting the creamy confections needed to run faster and further to get their treats.

Everyday, at the same time, Lenard patrolled these neighbourhoods. The children came out like ants at a picnic.

Lenard had gotten children to run down to the end of the street before he'd stop.

The next day, they turned the corner with him.

All the while their unsuspecting parents slowly conditioned, allowed their children out of their sights to buy their frozen treats.

Lenard could have his pick of flavours.

Dawn DeBraal lives in rural Wisconsin with her husband, two rat terriers, and a cat. She successfully raised two children (meaning they didn't return to the nest!) After many years serving the government at the Federal and County level, she recently retired. Having extra time on her hands she started to write after a paralyzed vocal cord took her ability to speak for two months. Not finding her voice, she discovered that her love of telling a good story could be written. Her works have been published in Palm-sized press, Spillwords, Mercurial Stories, Potato Soup Journal, and Blood Song Books.

Consume Me
by Jo Seysener

Her head rested upon the flagstones, cool beneath her neck. *Focus*.

Better that than on what was being extracted from her innards.

She ignored every tug, refusing to acknowledge the loss of the parts she knew the beast consumed.

It's for the best, the right thing to do. She breathed, not reduced to the blackness that threatened. Bile mixed with saliva pooled in her throat. Her sacrifice meant everything.

They would get away.

Her head lolled. Bright blue gazed back, reflecting no image, no life. Then came the pain. Tearing, ripping. Juices flowing into her hands, staining the flagstones beneath.

Jo Seysener is a mum of three crazies, a scatter of chickens, a decrepit kelpie and a rambunctious GSD. She lives with her husband near Brisbane, Australia. When she is not exposing her kids to cult story books from her childhood, she can be found in the kitchen experimenting with new flavours and pairings. She adores alpacas.
Facebook: joseysener
Website: www.joseysener.com

Ghouls
by Patrick Winters

Barnes handed the boy a shovel. "Get to it, lad. The university likes 'em fresh."

The youth gave a troubled look at the tombstone before them, but he soon joined his benefactor in their morbid task. They worked for nearly an hour, hauling earth aside by the light of Barne's lantern. Finally, when they struck the coffin's top, they took a rest.

"Gruesome work," Barnes sighed.

"But good eating."

The two whirled about, seeing a pale, ghastly thing grinning down at them from above.

They screamed; and by the end of the night, they'd become part of a three-course meal.

Patrick Winters is a graduate of Illinois College in Jacksonville, IL, where he earned a Bachelor of Arts degree in English Literature and Creative Writing and achieved membership into Sigma Tau Delta, an international English honors society. Winters is now a proud member of the Horror Writers Association, and his work has been published in the likes of Sanitarium Magazine, Deadman's Tome, Trysts of Fate, and other such titles. A full list of his previous publications may be found at his author's site. Website: wintersauthor.azurewebsites.net/Publications/List

The Troll Potion
by Shawn M. Klimek

"How was being a troll?" asked the witch.

"Worth every penny!" I declared. "The strength to rip my enemies, limb from limb? Imperviousness to most weapons and a complete disguise to shield me from legal consequences?" I presented another bag of gold. "I'd like the same potion again, please."

She frowned, then warned, "You must remember, any new warts you acquired are permanent. I strongly recommend you wait before drinking another dose."

"I'll wait," I promised, and I meant it. But then, on the way home, I heard a baby crying, and the warts in my mouth began to water.

Shawn M. Klimek is the middle child of seven creative siblings, a globetrotting, U.S. military spouse, an internationally best-selling short-story writer, a poet, and butler to a Maltese. Almost one hundred of his stories or poems have been published in digital magazines or anthologies, including BHP's Deep Space and the first six books in the Dark Drabbles series.
Website: jotinthedark.blogspot.com
Facebook: shawnmklimekauthor

The Itch
by R.A. Goli

Scratch. Scratch. Scratch. Kate's skin itched constantly.

She peered at her arms, at the white swirls visible underneath the surface. The squiggles moved; some sort of parasite had invaded her body!

Mortified, she scratched harder, faster, until the skin ripped open, and blood dripped down her forearms, face, neck, and legs.

Small white balls dropped to the floor. Little worms curled up for protection. Kate gasped, watching in horrified awe as they began to unfurl. She stomped on them, only to have more fall, cascading down her body like rocks down a mountain.

She screamed.

The worm-creatures had human faces.

R.A. Goli is an Australian writer of horror, fantasy, and speculative short stories. In addition to writing, her interests include reading, gaming, the occasional walk, and annoying her dog, two cats, and husband. Check out her numerous publications including her fantasy novella, The Eighth Dwarf, and her collection of short stories, Unfettered;
Website: ragoliauthor.wordpress.com
Facebook: RAGoliAuthor

Bell Temps
by Stephen Smith

My cat's got a bell that makes noise wherever he goes. I leave my bedroom door open in case he wants to come in at night. From the bottom of the stairs I hear,

Jing-a-ling-ling.

Climbing up the steps on silent claws,

Jing-a-ling-ling.

In the hall, pawing towards my room,

Jing-a-ling-ling.

He bounds into my room and leaps onto my bed. He drags his belly across my face before curling around my head and revving his little motor. I reach up to scratch his neck and my fingers only find fur where his collar should be.

Jing-a-ling-ling…ling…ling, in my doorway.

Stephen Smith *is a Canadian communications professional who writes weird fiction in their spare time.*
Website: canadianslush.wordpress.com/content-table/invisible

Forsaking All Others
by D.M. Burdett

Urgent knocking woke Jaycee. She opened her eyes into the subdued light of the hotel room.

Dan, her husband—the surgeon—watched over her.

"Police! Open up!" More insistent banging.

She remembered the tangle of sheets, her yoga instructor, Dan's angry face.

A heart monitor blipped next to her. "What have you done?" she breathed, terrified.

"I don't like to share." His smile didn't touch his eyes.

The door exploded. Officers spilled into the room but faltered at the sight.

"A hemicorporectomy." Dan sneered. "I amputated your body below the waist."

Jaycee made a choking sound.

"No more screwing around."

First published in *Trembling with Fear*, 2019

D.M. Burdett initially roamed as an army brat, but now lives in Australia where she spends her days avoiding drop bears and killer spiders. She has published a Sci-Fi series, has short stories in various anthologies, and has published two children's series. She is currently working on the first book in a dystopian series.
Website: www.dmburdett.com
Facebook: DMBurdett

Malice
by Umair Mirxa

Medusa walked down the streets of Athens, malice in her heart and revenge on her mind. A dozen innocent victims had already fallen prey to her gaze, but she felt no remorse.

She turned a corner, and there she was at last, Athena.

"So, you finally found the courage to face me?"

"I can't allow you to hurt my citizens."

"What will you do, great protector?" snarled Medusa. "Turn them into hideous monsters, too?"

"No. I shall end your misery."

They lunged at each other, the goddess and the Gorgon, and Athena walked away with Medusa's head decorating her shield.

Umair Mirxa lives in Karachi, Pakistan. His first published story, 'Awareness', appeared on Spillwords Press. He has also had stories accepted for anthologies from Zombie Pirate Publishing, Blood Song Books, Fantasia Divinity Magazine and Publishing, and Iron Faerie Publishing. He is a massive J.R.R. Tolkien fan, and loves everything to do with fantasy and mythology. He enjoys football, history, music, movies, TV shows, and comic books, and wishes with all his heart that dragons were real.
Website: www.umairmirxa.com
Facebook: UMirxa12

You Know My Name
by Austin P. Sheehan

Deafening winds howl my name as I soar in the blood-red sky above Drežďany. The medieval city is crowded with people broken by a desperate war. Overlooking the eternal river, dark with the filth of the wretched masses, is the fortress where my ancient foe hides.

From the cursed abyss that is my domain, I attack, my blood alive with hate. As the spire of a cathedral rises to meet me, my anger erupts into a towering, incandescent wall of fire. Enraged and unstoppable, I burn the monsters from the city streets, sucking the very life out of the air.

Austin P. Sheehan is a writer of speculative fiction, a lover of language, literature and '90s TV. Armed with a psychology degree, he went into the world to study humanity, and now prefers the company of his wife and their greyhounds. He grew up in the valleys of Victoria's high country, and despite living in Melbourne, always feels at home amongst the mountains. You'll often find mountains in his stories, whether they're sci-fi, fantasy or alternative history.
Website: austinpsheehan.com
Twitter: @AustinPSheehan

Compulsion
by Rowanne S. Carberry

Lurking in the shadows he sees his prey. Stumbling out of the club, held up by a friend, her eyes are blurred by drink. The friend hails a taxi and when one pulls up; he slinks out of the shadows.

"Hey, I'll take her home," he compels the friend.

She looks at him with suspicion which melts away as she looks in his eyes.

"Ok," she says in a trance, pushing the girl into his arms, the friend jumps in the taxi.

Taking the girl to an empty alley, he plunges his fangs into her throat drinking down her blood.

Rowanne S. Carberry was born in England in 1990, where she stills lives now with her cat Wolverine. Rowanne has always loved writing, and her first poem was published at the age of 15, but her ambition has always been to help people. Rowanne studied at the University of Sunderland where she completed combined honours of Psychology with Drama. Rowanne writes to offer others an escape. Although Rowanne writes in varied genres each story or poem she writes will often have a darkness to it, which helped coin her brand, Poisoned Quill Writing – Wicked words from a poisoned quill.
Facebook: PoisonedQuillWriting
Instagram: @poisoned_quill_writing

A Trip to the Vanderbilt Museum

by Matthew M. Montelione

Darla and Teddy marvelled at the three-thousand-year-old Egyptian mummy.

"Who was she, exactly?" Darla asked their guide.

"We don't know. Few records survived from that time period. She was young when she died, we know that, at least."

Teddy saw the mummy move out of the corner of his eye. At least he thought he did. Darla and the guide did not notice, they were busy talking history.

Teddy stared at the mummy.

"Next room, Ted," Darla said as she grabbed his hand.

Teddy questioned himself as they left the stuffy room.

The wanting mummy turned her head towards them.

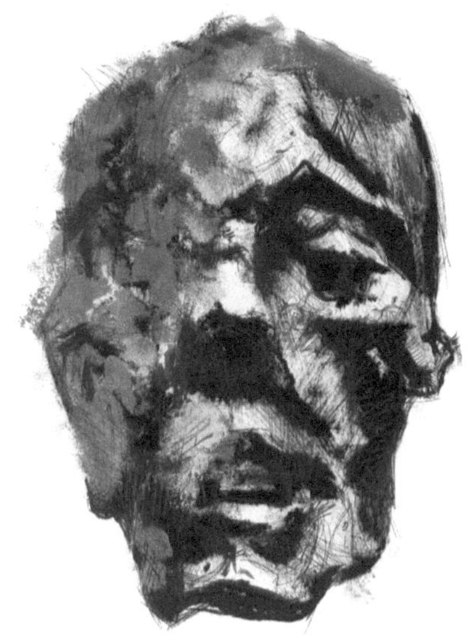

Matthew M. Montelione *is a horror writer born and raised on Long Island in New York. His stories have been published in Quoth the Raven: A Contemporary Reimagining of the Works of Edgar Allan Poe, Thuggish Itch: Devilish, MONSTERS: A Horror Microfiction Anthology, Eerie Christmas, and other titles. Matthew is also an American Revolution historian who focuses on the local experiences of Loyalists on Long Island. His work on the subject has been published in Long Island History Journal and Journal of the American Revolution. Matthew lives with his wife in New York.*
Website: maybeevils.com
Twitter: @maybeevils

7709
by Sinister Sweetheart

You could tell something was wrong with our house the second you stepped inside. Dark, plush carpet seemed to nip at the bottoms of your feet.

The walls appeared to breathe; expanding and retracting in the night. Flowered wallpaper ripped; its jagged edges like teeth. You mustn't walk too close to the edge of any room or hallway.

The groaning of pipes carry syllables in their sound. Conversations can be heard, and ethereal laughter is shared when no one is there.

When some houses settle, they creak and groan innocently, no threat lies within. When our house settles, it screams.

*Since **Sinister Sweetheart** made her first post to a popular Internet forum, she's taken the horror community by storm. Her ability to create, terrify, and drive home her stories is insurmountable. Sinister Sweetheart's published works can be found in multiple anthologies for all to read, but be forewarned, if you do... you may want to call your therapist after, her stories are terrifying, disturbing and devilishly unsettling. She is not only a fright visually, but also has a creepy tentacle in horror podcasting as well. Sinister Sweetheart writes, voice acts and is the media director of the Scarecrow Tales podcast.*
Website: Sinistersweetheart.wixsite.com/sinistersweetheart
Facebook: NMBrownStories

Morning Coffee
by J.M. Meyer

Joanne blew on the steaming coffee, scalding her tongue with the first sip. Placing the mug on the marble counter, she ran to her freezer for ice. Joanne pulled on the door which opened and shut as if someone played inside. She stopped when she spied long matted fur sticking out and around the closed door. Joanne stood in front of the Sub-Zero watching the silver door slowly open. A creature leaped out latching its razor-sharp teeth into her neck, pulling her through the freezer and freshly scratched hole that led to the outside world. Her coffee was still hot.

J.M. Meyer is writer, artist and small business owner living in New York., where she received her master's degree from Teacher's College, Columbia University. Jacqueline loves the science fiction and horror genres. Reading Ray Bradbury was a mind-blowing experience for her in 8th grade. Alfred Hitchcock and Rod Serling were the horror heroes of her youth. Mercedes M. Yardley is her current horror writing hero. Jacqueline also enjoys the company of her husband Bruce and their three children, Julia, Emma and Lauren. Jacqueline's mantra: The only time it's too late to try something new is when you are dead.
Website: jmoranmeyer.net
Twitter: @moran_meyer

Medusa's Den
by Pamela Jeffs

Stone is enduring, but the sea is incessant. She steals away from me those I love. Her salty touch invades my den, whispering fingers of water that wear away the edges of my stone creations. She takes their faces from me.

An insufferable theft.

The statue closest to the entrance is my most lamented lost. He was my first. The first adventurer to climb down the cliffs and look into my eyes.

The first to turn to stone.

The first to die.

I reach out and touch his cold cheek. My serpent hair hisses. Memory must suffice to remind me.

Pamela Jeffs *is a speculative fiction author living in Queensland, Australia with her husband and two daughters. She is a member of the Queensland Writers' Centre and has had numerous short fiction pieces published in recent national and international anthologies. In 2017 and again in 2018, Pamela was nominated for an Australian Aurealis Award in the category of 'Best Science Fiction Short Story'. Her debut collection titled 'Red Hour and Other Strange Tales' was released in March 2018.*
Website: www.pamelajeffs.com
Facebook: pamelajeffsauthor

Breakfast
by Nicole Little

We boarded up the windows and doors; in unison we hammered the final nails. The light was fading quickly, and we could not afford to waste time. I wound a length of thick chain through the door handle, securing it with a heavy lock. The shrieking and moaning begin as the sun plunged beneath the horizon; then the clawing and thrashing against the barriers.

"Do you think they'll be able to get out of there Pa?" I asked.

"Nah, they'll keep fine in there 'til mornin', son," he smiled in anticipation. "I haven't had long pig for breakfast in years."

Nicole Little is an award winning short story writer who lives in St. John's, Newfoundland, Canada. Her publishing credits to date include Sweet Sixteen (Kit Sora: The Artobiography, 2019), The Market (Dystopia from the Rock, 2019) and Last One Standing (Dystopia from the Rock, 2019). Her short story Doxxed placed favorably in the Writers Alliance of Newfoundland and Labrador's "A Nightmare on Water Street: Scary Story Reading". In her spare time, Nicole can be found with either a pen in her hand or her nose in a book. She is married with two daughters.

Who Else?
by R.G. Halstead

Wilbert walked out of church Sunday morning. He was going to make the world a better place.

As he sat in his car, waiting for everybody else to drive off, the religious man thought with a smile, *I am going to rid the world of vampires and zombies.*

As he drove off, Wilbert suddenly slammed on his brakes.

But what if somebody is offended by my killing these vile beasts? he asked himself. *They might...they **will** bring in lawyers to come down on me.*

Looking upward for guidance, Wilbert soon smiled again.

He would kill all the lawyers, too.

__R.G. Halstead__, a 63-year-old, takes to writing late in his life. Influences? Those old Alfred Hitchcock Mystery Magazines from the late 1950s and the 1960s with the great twisty endings. Love them.

Jack and Jill
by Brian Rosenberger

You know the story, the one where the two kids go up a hill to fetch a pail of water. They never tell you the whole truth, never mentioning the kids were into heavy metal, horror movies, always wore black, and dabbled in the occult. More than dabbled.

The brats actually summoned a demon. Their parents would have been proud. Had they survived. The demon incinerated them and the cottage. The kids fled in panic to the nearest water source. Too late.

How do I know? I was there and these hooves are capable of breaking a crown or two.

Brian Rosenberger lives in a cellar in Marietta, GA (USA) and writes by the light of captured fireflies. He is the author of As the Worms Turns and three poetry collections. He is also a featured contributor to the Pro-Wrestling literary collection, Three-Way Dance, available from Gimmick Press.
Facebook: HeWhoSuffers

Mumbling Monsters
by Gregg Cunningham

The ignorant called him Mumbles, the monster of the park, because of his constant drunken slur. The stench of urine followed him wherever he fell.

Kids were told by gossiping parents not to play in the park whenever Mumbles was around, and the police had moved the harmless drunk on so many times it was routine to get a call nowadays.

Fifteen years' military service had changed this once charming man into this homeless, alcoholic that nobody wanted to help.

They called him a damn disgrace.

Mumbles wept, only drinking to drown out the monsters constantly mumbling inside his head.

Gregg Cunningham 48, short story writer who has had to pick up his game since stumbling into facebook writer's groups. He has stories published by 559 Publishing in in 13 Bites volume 3,4,5, Plan 9 from Outer space, Other Realms, Heard It on The Radio, 559 Ways to Die, short stories publishing by Zombie Pirate Publishing in Relationship add Vice, Full Metal Horror, Phuket Tattoo, World War four and Flash Fiction Addiction (flash) with Zombie Pirate Publishing, and also in Daastan Magazine Chapter 11 and Brian,Rich and the Wardrobe.
Amazon: www.amazon.com/-/e/B016OTHX0K

Black Dog
by Raven Corinn Carluk

Cal zipped up and stumbled toward the large black dog that had followed him from the bar. "What the fuck do you want?" It simply stared with unblinking yellow eyes.

"Piss off!" He stooped and grabbed an empty bottle, flinging it at the mutt. The dog dodged to one side and continued to stare.

Cal's anger rose, and he chased after the thing, yelling obscenities. The dog finally ran, three steps ahead, looking over its shoulder the whole time.

The alley ended at a brick wall, forcing the dog to stop. Cal laughed. "Dumb mutt."

Six growls sounded behind him.

Raven Corinn Carluk is an indie author of dark fantasy and paranormal romance.
Website: RavenCorinnCarluk.Blogspot.Com

A Howling in the Moonlit Night
by E.L. Giles

"Tie me, my friend, as tightly as you can," I said, my eyes averting the ominous sight of the full moon rising.

The room grew colder and darker, pregnant with stark fear.

"And then what?" asked my friend, his voice strained with disbelief.

"And then run for your life, before it's too late, for the moon is full and bloody."

"Isn't there another way besides tying you up like a madman in a padded room?"

"None that would prevent the carnage to come."

The pressure grew within my core. The beast was close.

"Run!" I screamed. "Run, my dear friend!"

E.L. Giles is a dreamer, passionate about art, a restless worker and a bit of a weird human. He started his artistic journey as a music composer until the need to put his thoughts and stories down on paper grew too strong for him to resist it any longer. He lives in the French Province of Quebec, Canada, with his girlfriend and two boys.
Facebook: elgilesauthor
Website: www.elgilesauthor.com

Shreds
by Michael D. Lackey

How do you stop an animal you can't see? How do you go about a normal day not knowing if it will be your last?

The town of Hyde, New York is on high alert. Human remains—well shreds of flesh—have been found in multiple locations. The army had to be called in and they prove to be just added food for the monster they call Jeckle. Nightfall is its playground, covered by darkness the monster stalks its prey. Screams split the silence of sleep. Awakened by fright, paralyzed by knowledge.

Jeckle of Hyde transforming this town into Hell.

Michael D. Lackey is a fantasy and Sci-fi writer. He is the author of The Bad Seed: Battle for the Heavens and The Key of Knowledge. He enjoys creating worlds for new readers and old to escape to and just have fun.
Website: www.michaellackeyauthor.com

Ivie's Bubble Bath
by Gabriella Balcom

Pouring lavender-scented bubble bath into her bathtub, Ivie turned on the hot water and grabbed a facecloth.

A dark object no bigger than a BB came out of the faucet with the water, then a second. Dozens followed, all concealed beneath the bubbles.

Ivie hadn't noticed anything unusual. Humming, she turned off the water and climbed into the tub. She leaned back, then shot upright. "What the...?" She'd felt movement by her leg.

Seeing tiny, glowing eyes in the liquid surrounding her, Ivie shrieked. The unknown creatures stung her again and again. Losing consciousness, her head slipped below the water.

***Gabriella Balcom** lives in Texas with her family, loves reading and writing, and thinks she was born with a book in her hands. She works in a mental health field, and writes fantasy, horror/thriller, romance, children's stories, and sci-fi. She likes travelling, music, good shows, photography, history, interesting tales, and animals. Gabriella says she's a sucker for a great story and loves forests, mountains, and back roads which might lead who knows where. She has a weakness for lasagne, garlic bread, tacos, cheese, and chocolate, but not necessarily in that order.*
Facebook: GabriellaBalcom.lonestarauthor

Bed Bug
by Dawn DeBraal

David watched as the crawly thing scurried under his bed.

"Mom!" he screamed out. His mother came into his room again.

"What now, David?" He pointed under the bed pulling his covers up to his nose.

"I saw it again." he cried, his lip quivering. His mother got down on her knees waving her arms back and forth under the bed. Nothing happened, nothing scurried out.

"See David, there is nothing here. You don't have to be afraid. I'm looking under your bed now. Hello?" his mother called out.

That's when the crawly thing pulled David's mother under the bed.

Dawn DeBraal lives in rural Wisconsin with her husband, two rat terriers, and a cat. She successfully raised two children (meaning they didn't return to the nest!) After many years serving the government at the Federal and County level, she recently retired. Having extra time on her hands she started to write after a paralyzed vocal cord took her ability to speak for two months. Not finding her voice, she discovered that her love of telling a good story could be written. Her works have been published in Palm-sized press, Spillwords, Mercurial Stories, Potato Soup Journal, and Blood Song Books.

A Taste of Vetala Vengeance
by Chitra Gopalakrishnan

I, a *vetala*, linger with febrile intensity in a graveyard. To unleash terror by entering a dead body.

The grass mirrors my unease, crackling under a malevolent sun.

An abrupt pause in its rustling shows me three men. They lay a dead woman on the pyre's dry surface and leave in indecent haste before she is pyre-burnt.

My muscles spiral with joy. I know her flesh won't catch fire and fall away to allow her spirit fly free.

I can keep this one, who studied death lore in her life, in my twilight zone—between life and after-life. '

Forever.

Chitra Gopalakrishnan is a journalist by training, a social development communications consultant by profession and a creative writer by choice. Chitra's focus is on issues of gender, environment and health. Chitra dabbles in poetry on the sly and literary creations openly on the web using social media.
Website: unpublishedplatform.weebly.com/chitra-gopalakrishnan

Cellar Beware
by Liam Hogan

Noises beyond the cellar door. Tommy thought about snuffing the flame but relighting the candle in the dark would be tricky. The something slithered closer.

Knock!

"Don't ever go out," his dad always growled. "Even if hungry. The people—things—above, they're not like us."

Knock-knock!

They'd agreed a pattern, to identify friend from foe.

Knock.

Tommy slid the bolts, turned the keys, struggled with the metal rod, their last defence. He swung the heavy door. In the gloom a hunched form clutched a dripping sack of misshapen lumps.

"Hi, Dad," Tommy grinned through pointed teeth, "Got something for me?"

Liam Hogan is a London based short story writer, the host of Liars' League, and a Ministry of Stories mentor. His story "Ana", appears in Best of British Science Fiction 2016 (NewCon Press) and his twisted fantasy collection, "Happy Ending Not Guaranteed", is published by Arachne Press. Website: happyendingnotguaranteed.blogspot.co.uk Twitter: @LiamJHogan

The Ropen
by Sinister Sweetheart

People rush to the underground tunnels at the sound of the alarm, clutching their children tight.

Feeding time's earlier than expected, and the island's unprepared. The Ropen's screech roars throughout the night.

A bat with devil eyes and a twenty-foot wingspan. It favours human blood and is under the impression that the Island belongs to it. Most people make it to shelter safely.

Across the barren lot, you see Nona, an elderly wise woman recovering from a fall. She has no family to help her. The bat chomps her in its jaws before she even knows she's off the ground.

*Since **Sinister Sweetheart** made her first post to a popular Internet forum, she's taken the horror community by storm. Her ability to create, terrify, and drive home her stories is insurmountable. Sinister Sweetheart's published works can be found in multiple anthologies for all to read, but be forewarned, if you do... you may want to call your therapist after, her stories are terrifying, disturbing and devilishly unsettling. She is not only a fright visually, but also has a creepy tentacle in horror podcasting as well. Sinister Sweetheart writes, voice acts and is the media director of the Scarecrow Tales podcast.*
Website: Sinistersweetheart.wixsite.com/sinistersweetheart
Facebook: NMBrownStories

Below Bob's Bed
by J.M. Meyer

Bob slept to the familiar sound of scratching below his floor. He dozed in and out until the eerie quiet jolted him out of bed before sunrise. Bob pushed his four-poster bed aside and rolled up the antique carpet, exposing a latched door. Forgetting he had locked it, Bob found the skeleton key, under his Bible, in the top drawer. Click. Expecting to see his latest expired victim, he instead met the gaze of the beautiful pale woman he abducted from the bus stop six days ago. She laughed, exposing her large canines, before sinking them into Bob's doughy flesh.

J.M. Meyer is writer, artist and small business owner living in New York., where she received her master's degree from Teacher's College, Columbia University. Jacqueline loves the science fiction and horror genres. Reading Ray Bradbury was a mind-blowing experience for her in 8th grade. Alfred Hitchcock and Rod Serling were the horror heroes of her youth. Mercedes M. Yardley is her current horror writing hero. Jacqueline also enjoys the company of her husband Bruce and their three children, Julia, Emma and Lauren. Jacqueline's mantra: The only time it's too late to try something new is when you are dead.
Website: jmoranmeyer.net
Twitter: @moran_meyer

Fae
by K.T. Tate

Mommy doesn't believe me but there are fairies under the bed. I've seen them. They are like mice, but they have people hands and no tail. I wanted to be friends but one of them hissed at me so now I just watch them.

Tonight, I woke up just in time to see them leaving my room. I follow them hoping for adventure. Instead, they are going into Mommy's room. Perhaps now she'll believe me.

I approach the bed, but the blanket starts to writhe. White sheets stain red. Tears well up instantly as I start to scream. They're burrowing.

K.T. Tate lives in Cambridgeshire in the UK. She writes mainly weird fiction, cosmic horror and strange monster stories.
Website: eldritchhollow.wordpress.com
Tumblr: eldritch-hollow.tumblr.com

Her Dominion
by Charlotte O'Farrell

She could take over the bodies of almost every person in the western world at will. She could make them say and do anything she wanted. Her power over politics, economics and culture was absolute, and she wasn't shy about it.

And all due to that silly myth that made parents put teeth under their kids' pillows. She was no fairy; any child who woke up and saw her true form would die of horror, but she was careful not to wake them.

She left a pound coin, but it wasn't just their teeth she took. It was their soul.

Charlotte O'Farrell is a lifelong horror fan who writes about all manner of the weird and wonderful. Her work can be found at the Drabble, the Rock N Roll Horror Zine and Horror Tree, among other places.
Twitter: @ChaOFarrell

Coffin Mates
by Terry Miller

I had a dream that I walked amongst the dead. I awoke, my body shivering as if I brought the cold out with me. My limbs were stiff, and the room was dark and damp. Attempting to move, I banged both my elbows; the sudden, numbing pain being anything but humorous.

Panicking, I found myself surrounded on every side, and the air I frantically breathed grew thin. Fingers clawed at my shirt, ripping it bottom to top. My stomach soured as rank breath exhaled onto my face. Something had followed me back, its frigid, bony fingers slipping under my skin.

Terry Miller *is an author and 2017 Rhysling Award-nominated poet residing in Portsmouth, OH, USA. He has self-published a dark poetry collection on Amazon and one short story to date. His work has also appeared in Sanitarium, Devolution Z, Jitter Press, Poetry Quarterly, O Unholy Night in Deathlehem, and the 2017 Rhysling Anthology from the Science Fiction and Fantasy Poetry Association.*
Facebook: tmiller2015

A Monster? Not I
by Alexander Pyles

There was blood on the floor. Mine?

Memories of coming home, seeing the children, my wife, and then…nothing.

I wracked my brain for more, something else, anything else, but there was only the sight of blood drying on the hardwood.

I needed to leave, get away from it, but part of me was compelled. The sickly sweetness of death forced me to stay. My mouth watered. This had to be what I wanted.

I noticed the dyed headband, lying there amid a pool of red. Once white, it was now a dull brown.

My heart beat with fresh blood.

Alexander Pyles resides in IL with his wife and children. He holds an MA in Philosophy and an MFA in Writing Popular Fiction. His short story chapbook titled, "Milo (01001101 01101001 01101100 01101111)," from Radix Media, is due out fall 2019. His other short fiction has appeared on 101fiction.org, River and South Review, and other venues. Website: www.pylesofbooks.com
Twitter: @Pylesofbooks

The Child of the Night
by E.L. Giles

Deep down in the very guts of Earth were catacombs, galleries of the mutilated and the dismembered, the martyrs and the saints.

Old Roman ruins they were, vaulted warrens and corridors, darker than the darkest night itself. But what truth remained within these rocky tombs was the holy pain inhabiting the pestilent caves and crawling out through every crack in the walls. Plague, it seemed, festered beneath the surface.

The strained souls and ghoulish shapes floated like a miasmatic cloud, poisonous and murderous, vengeful and evil, contaminating the very essence of life and condemning everything that once walked this world.

E.L. Giles *is a dreamer, passionate about art, a restless worker and a bit of a weird human. He started his artistic journey as a music composer until the need to put his thoughts and stories down on paper grew too strong for him to resist it any longer. He lives in the French Province of Quebec, Canada, with his girlfriend and two boys.*
Facebook: elgilesauthor
Website: www.elgilesauthor.com

Death Metal
by Steven Holding

It's no new gimmick; heavy thrash from men in make-up, but they rock.

She writhes to the killer riffs, ears nearly bleeding at the screaming vocals volume. Strobe lights throw razor shadows, the musicians twisted features illuminated; scaled skin, fangs, horns, forked tongues.

The set ends in frenzied destruction.

Backstage, amongst the druggies and groupies, she finds the frontman. Blows his ego with inflated praise. Yanks him through the fire exit; pleases him on her knees in the damp, deserted alleyway.

Rising, hands caress as she tries to kiss his face.

Then the scream as his mask stays in place.

Steven Holding lives with his family in the United Kingdom. His stories have been published by TREMBLING WITH FEAR, FRIDAY FLASH FICTION, THEATRE CLOUD, AD HOC FICTION and MASSACRE MAGAZINE. Most recently, his story THREE CHORDS AND THE TRUTH received first place in the INKTEARS 2018 FLASH FICTION COMPETITION, while another of his pieces WALK WITH ME THROUGH THE LONG GRASS AND I SHALL HOLD YOUR HAND was runner up in the annual WRITING MAGAZINE 500 WORD SHORT STORY COMPETITION. He is currently working upon further short fiction and a novel.
Website: www.stevenholding.co.uk

Mingo Motel is a Killhouse
by Jacob Baugher

The bone shards were Dexter's favourite part. They snapped between his rabid jigsaw teeth. He slurped soggy intestines like sluggy noodles. Smeared bile across his tarantula beard. He was a rawhead, after all.

Yesterday's housekeeper stained hotel room's bed. All the fun fluid spattered the ceiling. It rocketed from the aorta when he tore through her with a broken mop handle. Punctured her belly and rolled in the juices. Now her ghost vomited ectoplasm in the corner trash can.

Someone knocked at the door.

"Housekeeping."

Dexter put his human face on; opened the door.

"Thank God. Someone's made a mess."

Jacob Baugher teaches Creative Writing at Franciscan University of Steubenville. When he's not teaching or coaching the track team, he can be found in the Cuyahoga Valley hiking with his wife and son or brewing beer on his front porch. He's received honourable mentions for his work in the Writers of the Future contest and he co-edits a series of Fantasy and Science Fiction anthologies titled Continuum.

Never Talk to Strangers
by Aiki Flinthart

"Watch for him, Cath," my sister said. "It's the third rape this month. Pretends to be a tradesman."

I rolled my eyes.

The doorbell chimed.

"Gotta go, Jilly." I hung up.

Behind the door waited a man who made my heart skip. Tall. Dark-haired. Winter-sky eyes that slid the length of my body. His white smile widened.

"May I come in, ma'am?" He flashed an ID card. "Here to check a gas leak."

I let him in. "Glad you came."

"Me too." One hand grabbed my throat. "Don't scream."

"Oh, no." I smiled, showing fangs. "Same goes for you, though."

Aiki Flinthart has had short stories shortlisted in the Aurealis awards and top-8 listed in the USA Writers of the Future competition, as well as published in various anthologies and e-mags. She has 11 published spec fic novels and has edited 2 short story anthologies. She regularly gives workshops on writing fight scenes at conventions. Lives in Brisbane. Does martial arts, archery, knife throwing and lute-playing.
Website: www.aikiflinthart.com

Broken
by David Bowmore

In his mind he saw a young man's face, but whenever he caught his reflection in a stream, he would wonder whose face he wore now.

His hands came from another too, a manual worker by the look of them. Why was the stitching so rough?

Because one leg was shorter than the other, each leg being from different men, he would forever have a limp. Did not the madman care for the creature that would have to walk around with them?

And the less said about what should have been in his britches, the better.

He could still cry.

David Bowmore has lived here, there and everywhere, but now lives in Yorkshire with his wonderful wife and a small white poodle. He has worn many hats in his time; head chef, teacher and landscape gardener. His first collection of short stories 'The Magic of Deben Market' is available from Clarendon House.
Website: davidbowmore.co.uk
Facebook: davidbowmoreauthor

Howl
by Andrew Anderson

Standing at the top of the mountain at midnight, he could feel the moon begin to affect his body; his arms, incisors and nails lengthened, thick fur started to grow upon his body and as his muscles increased mass, his clothes were torn away.

He looked down at the unsuspecting village which was spread out like an illuminated blanket below him. As if scripted, before proceeding to wreak untold havoc on its townsfolk, he knew what came next.

However, looking up caused him confusion: there were five moons which circled this planet.

Howl to the moon, but to which one?

Andrew Anderson is a full-time civil servant, dabbling in writing music, poetry, screenplays and short stories in his limited spare time, when not working on building himself a fort made out of second-hand books. He lives in Bathgate, Scotland with his wife, two children and his dog.
Twitter: @soorploom

Below the Waves
by Crystal L. Kirkham

Beneath the endless waves. Deep down in those unexplored depths, they remained hidden. Relegated to nothing more than myth and legend by modern man. They passed the time sharpening tooth and claw, knowing that it would be needed

When the oceans rose against the land, they surged forth to destroy what little remained of the landwalkers that had poisoned their home. And to show them that they were not the gorgeous fish-tailed men and women that legends told of. They were warriors and they were angry.

They did not stop until none of their enemy remained; the planet was theirs.

Crystal L. Kirkham *resides in a small hamlet west of Red Deer, Alberta. She's an avid outdoors person, unrepentant coffee addict, part-time foodie, servant to a wonderful feline, and companion to two delightfully hilarious canines. She will neither confirm nor deny the rumours regarding the heart in a jar on her desk and the bottle of reader's tears right next to it. Her paranormal urban fantasy series, Saints and Sinners, is available on Amazon and her YA Fantasy, Feathers and Fae will be released October 11, 2019, from Kyanite Publishing.*
Website: www.crystallkirkham.com

Truth Behind the Façade
by J.U. Menon

They say everyone has two faces. One that they put on—the façade—and another that stays hidden—the true face.

"Let me out!" screamed the latter as Dan headed towards the bathroom. "I can't breathe."

"You have to stay hidden," Dan replied. "No one can know you exist."

"Please, just for a minute. I am suffocating!"

Dan sighed and stopped by the mirror to take off the façade. He watched as huge boils began to erupt all over the face beneath it.

"You will NEVER conceal me again," the monster's true face shrieked maniacally. "I am free at last!"

J.U. Menon is a scientist living in Rhode Island, USA, and is currently working on her young adult novel. She writes fantasy and science fiction while occasionally dabbling in dark fiction and poetry.
Twitter: @ju_menon
Instagram: @iam_jumenon

Monsteropolis Will Bleed
by Joshua D. Taylor

There will be a rumble in the streets of Monsteropolis tonight. The Killer Klowns and The Mad Mummiez are going to settle things for good. The streets will run red with blood. And blue, and green, and black.

The Klowns polish their big red shoes while the Mummiez tighten their wrappings. Whoever survives will be the new kings of the Southside.

The Diabolical Diablos watch with amusement from the fire and brimstone of the Eastside. Parents gather up their banshees and ghouls as monstrous gangsters flood the streets from basements and alleyways like backed up sewage.

Tonight, Monsteropolis will bleed.

Joshua D. Taylor is an amateur writer who started writing a few years ago when he realised he was too old to play make-believe. He lives in southeastern Pennsylvania with his wife and a one-eared cat. He enjoys gardening, comic books, ska-punk music, Disney World, and travelling with his wife. Raised during weirdness that was the late 20th century Josh's eclectic interests produce eclectic works. He loves to mix-n-match things from different genres and stories elements to achieve a madcap hodgepodge of the truly unexpected. His short story 'the Obelisk' appears in Salty Tales by Stormy Island Publishing.
Facebook: authorjoshuadtaylor

Swimming
by Vonnie Winslow Crist

After hiking to Blackwater Lake, perspiration dampened Sue's back. Rather than wait for friends, she decided to swim alone in the hemlock-stained water.

Dragonflies buzzing nearby, she removed sandals, then waded in. Sue noticed bubbles bursting on the surface a few meters away, wondered what sort of fish created them.

Suddenly, a horse's head lifted from the water—its eyes imploring her to paddle closer.

When she obediently drew alongside the kelpie, the urge to ride the waterhorse was overwhelming. Once astride the beast, Sue couldn't dismount—even when the monster plunged to the lake's bottom.

She didn't drown quickly.

Vonnie Winslow Crist is author of The Enchanted Dagger, Owl Light, The Greener Forest, Murder on Marawa Prime, and other award-winning books. Her fiction is included in "Amazing Stories," "Cast of Wonders," "Outposts of Beyond," Killing It Softly 2, Defending the Future - Dogs of War, Midnight Masquerade, Chaos of Hard Clay, and elsewhere. A cloverhand who has found so many four-leafed clovers she keeps them in jars, Vonnie strives to celebrate the power of myth in her writing.
Website: www.vonniewinslowcrist.com

Old Joe
by John Saxton

Cops didn't have a single lead.

He took the first with a smashed beer bottle; godawful jagged edges taking an eye, opening the jugular. Old dolt deserved it, farting away like a skunk!

Latest bought it with a biro, hard into the ear-canal, hearing-aid busted, so it couldn't whistle no more.

Old Joe's new neighbour in the home plays violin—badly.

The nurse pities Joe, dribbling in his vegetative state.

She turns away. His eyes flash with anticipation.

Kingshit next door fiddles on; soon to be silenced.

Old Joe grins, raises himself up, the centuries-old pretence dropped once more.

John Saxton hails from Yorkshire, UK, where he is happily married, with two sons. He has had over 50 short horror stories published in the independent press, including his own collection: 'Bloodshot'. He writes mainly after dark...
Twitter: @jsaxtonwriter

Renovating
by Raven Corinn Carluk

Dieter was a young city planner, hungry to bring Aachen into the modern era. Freshen the German city, let it reflect new multi-cultural standards.

First thing to go was this ugly Bahkauv statue.

He watched with glee as the bronze monstrosity was uprooted by the crane. Dieter had stared at the mutant calf and its rat tail while growing up, and the relief he felt was instantaneous. Good riddance.

Vapours rose from the ancient well below, then coalesced into a giant disfigured calf, slime covered. Red eyes bulged from its misshapen skull while it screamed its rage.

Dieter's bladder released.

Raven Corinn Carluk is an indie author of dark fantasy and paranormal romance.
Website: RavenCorinnCarluk.Blogspot.Com

Moon Cursed
by Zoey Xolton

Serena sobbed into the darkness of her grandparent's basement. The dank odour of rot and damp permeated her sparse living quarters as the swamp above tried to erode the old plantation manor's foundations. How foolish she had been to venture alone into the night, even after she'd been forbidden.

She had broken Council Law. Now she was cursed, like the others who vanished every Full Moon to stalk the moors and quiet town of Northshire; except that she was not free to roam as her brothers and sisters were. She was trapped and left to face her inner beast alone.

Zoey Xolton is an Australian Speculative Fiction writer, primarily of Dark Fantasy, Paranormal Romance and Horror. She is also a proud mother of two and is married to her soul mate. Outside of her family, writing is her greatest passion. She is especially fond of short fiction and is working on releasing her own themed collections in future.
Website: www.zoeyxolton.com

Mermaid
by Jill Hand

I'm swimming when they first see me, moving easily through the water. They think I'm a seal and bring the boat closer. If there's more than one man in the boat I vanish, diving deep, letting them wonder.

But if there is one man I wait. I can see his surprise as he takes in my face. Nothing about it frightens them. Not all predators look frightening, not at first.

I raise my arms, as if asking to be lifted into the boat. By the time they notice the shimmering grey scales below my waist it's too late. They're mine.

Jill Hand is from New Jersey, USA. She is a member of the Horror Writers Association and International Thriller Writers. Her work has appeared in many anthologies, including Mrs. Rochester's Attic, The Shadow Booth, Vol. 3 and Caravans Awry, among others. She is the author of the Southern Gothic thriller, White Oaks, which has been praised by reviewers for its humor, memorable characters, and unexpected plot twists.
Website: www.jillhandauthor.com

Imps
by David Bowmore

Imps. Thousands of tiny monsters from the realm of nightmares.

Flying in packs of fifty or more and striking in the dead of night.

No one has seen them since the early dark ages, when they were defeated by prayer and magic.

More people are reporting sightings with every passing day. And by sightings, I mean attacks.

The victims always die from the thousands of tiny bite marks they receive. With every death, more imp sightings are reported.

The government has declared martial law and advises citizens to stay inside, keeping windows and doors locked.

And pray to your God.

David Bowmore *has lived here, there and everywhere, but now lives in Yorkshire with his wonderful wife and a small white poodle. He has worn many hats in his time; head chef, teacher and landscape gardener. His first collection of short stories 'The Magic of Deben Market' is available from Clarendon House.*
Website: davidbowmore.co.uk
Facebook: davidbowmoreauthor

The Beast of Hillfort
by Graham Robert Scott

The Beast of Hillfort wasn't, as generally assumed, a dragon, though it had a sharkworth of teeth and a murder of wings.

It didn't spit fire, though other creatures passing by in the night sometimes did.

It had no particular taste for virgins, though in droughts of its preferred game, if the village didn't offer up easy snacks, it would go on a bit of a rampage, level buildings, grab oxen from the fields.

Yet the Beast's preferred game, when it could be found, was dragon.

The village learned this the hard way, after they found someone to kill it.

Graham Robert Scott writes tales that are wry, dark, and speculative. He's published science-fiction in Nature, horror in Barrelhouse Online, and really tiny stories in 50-Word Stories and on his Twitter feed. His personal website takes its name from the prehistoric bear-dog, a toothy hunter that (like the platypus) couldn't quite make up its mind what it was. As a college professor by day and creative writer by night, Graham identifies.
Website: hemicyon.wordpress.com
Twitter: @graythebruce

The Tower Bell
by Claire Wilson

6am

The blue tinge to her skin, the girl's headphones fused with her face meant she'd been dead a while. Some maniac had ripped out the girl's throat. The strange thing? There was no blood.

"Have you taken a statement?"

"Yes. He didn't see anything, Sir."

9.50pm

She ran past the tower bell, turning up the volume.

10pm

Hunger motivated me into the night. I saw her. Headphones so loud I could hear the song. You had to be careful with athletic ones. She'd be able to throw a decent punch.

Checking her pulse turned out to be her downfall.

Claire Wilson has been writing professionally for seven years. She has been published in anthologies on several occasions. She has written over 100 short stories as well as working on a seven-book crime series and is actively seeking representation.
Twitter: @byclairewilson

Skinwalker
by Brandy Bonifas

The elders wouldn't speak of skinwalkers for fear of attracting one, but we were young and foolish. We sought out Old Man Crabtree. He loved to talk, filling our heads with lore.

Bored, we drove the dirt road he mentioned in stories, hoping to see for ourselves. Tires screeched, halting. A coyote glared into our headlights…with human eyes.

We returned to Crabtree's to tell him what we'd seen. We noticed the coyote pelt discarded on his floor just before Crabtree greeted us…with coyote eyes and canine teeth.

In the distance, a band of coyotes joined in our screams.

Brandy Bonifas lives in Ohio with her husband and son. Her work has appeared or is forthcoming in anthologies by Clarendon House Publications, Pixie Forest Publishing, Zombie Pirate Publishing, and Blood Song Books, as well as the online publications CafeLit and Spillwords Press.
Website: www.brandybonifas.com
Facebook: brandybonifasauthor

Memento
by J. Farrington

I know you. I know everything there is to know about you. How are you enjoying the stories so far? Sending shivers down your spine yet? I knew you would be reading this, so I thought I'd give you a chance.

I've been watching since you were little, from the shadows. I live amongst the damp, and the mould behind your boiler...collecting those discarded bits of trash, leftovers, even those strands of loose hair and nasty toenail clippings you leave behind.

The thing is, they don't satisfy me anymore; I need more than a memento.

I'm coming, for you.

J. Farrington is an aspiring author from the West Midlands, UK. His genre of choice is horror; whether that be psychological, suspense, supernatural or straight up weird, he'll give it a shot! He has loved writing from a young age but has only publicly been spreading his darker thoughts and sinister imagination via social platforms since 2018. If you would like to view his previous work, or merely lurk in the shadows...watching, you can keep up to date with future projects by spirit board or alternatively, the following;
Twitter: @SurvivorTrench
Reddit: TrenchChronicles

Ground Demons
by Matthew M. Montelione

Jeremiah Graham was jogging when he tripped on a branch and landed in thorns. He looked back and noticed that the branch was actually a leg, attached to a body that rose from the dirt. The creature towered over him, its curved horns protruded from its forehead.

"The humans will pay for their sins against the Earth," the demon said. Its diamond eyes fell on Jeremiah. "But you… for your blood sacrifice, shall serve us."

Jeremiah was badly cut and felt blood trickling down his legs. He convulsed and transformed into a horned beast.

"Rise, Ground Demon!" the beast bellowed.

Matthew M. Montelione is a horror writer born and raised on Long Island in New York. His stories have been published in Quoth the Raven: A Contemporary Reimagining of the Works of Edgar Allan Poe, Thuggish Itch: Devilish, MONSTERS: A Horror Microfiction Anthology, Eerie Christmas, and other titles. Matthew is also an American Revolution historian who focuses on the local experiences of Loyalists on Long Island. His work on the subject has been published in Long Island History Journal and Journal of the American Revolution. Matthew lives with his wife in New York.
Website: maybeevils.com
Twitter: @maybeevils

The Deal
by Donald Jacob Uitvlugt

Leaves rustle.

"Most unusual." Northrop touches the knot. "The sap looks like…blood."

The bark-covered pustule oozes, coating Northrop's fingers. He can't pull them away.

"Denis, a little help."

The sap burns. The knot sucks down his hand to the wrist.

"Denis!"

"Sorry, professor. Had to get a shovel."

As Northrop turns, Denis bashes his head in. It takes him the rest of the afternoon to dismember the body and bury it at the base of the tree. He wipes his brow and then looks up to the topmost branches.

"One more and you let my brother go, right?"

Leaves rustle.

First appeared online in The Horror Tree, 2013

Donald Jacob Uitvlugt lives on neither coast of the United States, but mostly in a haunted memory palace of his own design. His short fiction has appeared in numerous print and online venues, including Cirsova Magazine and the Flame Tree Press anthology Murder Mayhem. He works primarily in speculative fiction, though he loves blending and stretching genres. He strives to write what he calls "haiku fiction," stories that are small in scale but big in impact. Website: haikufiction.blogspot.com Twitter: @haikufictiondju

Mid-Eclipse
by Vonnie Winslow Crist

Dying to watch the moon turn red, before sleep, I set my alarm for mid-eclipse. But instead of ringing, I awake to my dog's howls.

I kneel beside her, and we both stare out the glass door at the bloody moon.

Hair on the backs of our necks rise as a terrible howling comes from the backyard and we spot a dark shape racing toward us.

My dog is quicker than me—she scrambles for cover, leaving me to face the furred obscenity on the other side of the door.

Possessing no silver bullets, I await breaking glass and teeth.

Vonnie Winslow Crist is author of The Enchanted Dagger, Owl Light, The Greener Forest, Murder on Marawa Prime, and other award-winning books. Her fiction is included in "Amazing Stories," "Cast of Wonders," "Outposts of Beyond," Killing It Softly 2, Defending the Future - Dogs of War, Midnight Masquerade, Chaos of Hard Clay, and elsewhere. A cloverhand who has found so many four-leafed clovers she keeps them in jars, Vonnie strives to celebrate the power of myth in her writing.
Website: www.vonniewinslowcrist.com

From Alfred Fanshawe's Travel Journal – Final Entry, 1883
by Aiki Flinthart

Dearest Emmaline,

After three weeks, we have found the island. I know you think it wicked, but I am about to emulate Odysseus. The sailors wear earplugs and will tie me to the mast.

The sky is thunderous, the Mediterranean rough. But I foresee no problems. I don't truly believe sirens are real. Or that their song is mesmerising, as the fables say.

I hear music in the distance. Probably some islander tricking us.

But I'll go and be tied.

Perhaps I'll take a small knife. Just in case I need to cut the ropes in an emergency.

Yours

Alfred

Aiki Flinthart *has had short stories shortlisted in the Aurealis awards and top-8 listed in the USA Writers of the Future competition, as well as published in various anthologies and e-mags. She has 11 published spec fic novels and has edited 2 short story anthologies. She regularly gives workshops on writing fight scenes at conventions. Lives in Brisbane. Does martial arts, archery, knife throwing and lute-playing.*
Website: www.aikiflinthart.com

The Wechuge
by Patrick Winters

Enli was once the greatest hunter of his people. Now, he preyed on what remained of them.

The last three men stood in a circle amidst the ruins of their village, spears held in blind defence against the whipping snow. Grunts echoed from all around; there was a reek in the air; and a towering shadow circled within the haze.

As the wind struck up again, the first man was disembowelled; a moment later, the second fell dead in the drifts, without his head.

The third shut his eyes, prayed—and then he was carried off, screaming into the white.

Patrick Winters is a graduate of Illinois College in Jacksonville, IL, where he earned a Bachelor of Arts degree in English Literature and Creative Writing and achieved membership into Sigma Tau Delta, an international English honors society. Winters is now a proud member of the Horror Writers Association, and his work has been published in the likes of Sanitarium Magazine, Deadman's Tome, Trysts of Fate, and other such titles. A full list of his previous publications may be found at his author's site. Website: wintersauthor.azurewebsites.net/Publications/List

Garbage
by Jacek Wilkos

John grimaced with disapproval. The trash bin was full again. Fortunately, the building had a garbage chute. He took out the bag and left the apartment.

The room was dark. When John approached the metal flap, something opened it from the inside. He felt a slimy tentacle wrapping around his legs, torso, neck. He heard the sound of crushing bones as he was being pulled into the chute. He flew through the gullet several meters.

Rusty mouth opened on each floor, with a huge tongue crawling out.

It was hungry and leftovers were no longer enough. It needed fresh meat.

Jacek Wilkos is an engineer from Poland. He lives with his wife and daughter in a beautiful city of Cracow. He writes mostly horror drabbles. His fiction in Polish can be read on Szortal, Niedobre literki, Horror Online. Lately he started translating his stories into English with the hope of publishing them.
Facebook: Jacek.W.Wilkos

The Circle
by Jem McCusker

The flesh of the black crow—a most succulent treat—is to be savoured. I lick my lips, once, twice and to complete the union, thrice. From the first spill of blood to the sharp crack of fine bone, I rejoice as I inhale the scent of rotting meat. The fire sparks to life in the makeshift hearth and the chorus of the dead claw at my feet, their faces a mixture of horror and awe. I leave my throne and walk amongst them as their souls' quiver in fear. Alas, the circle is complete, for now they are mine.

Jem McCusker is a middle grade fiction author, living near Brisbane with her two sons and husband. Her first book Stone Guardians the Rise of Eden was released in 2018 and she is working on the sequel. She is releasing a Novella for the Four Quills writing group, A Storm of Wind and Rain series in July, 2019. She longs to be a full-time author, won't wear yellow and loves rabbits. Follow Jem on Twitter, Facebook and Instagram. Details on her website.
Website: www.jemmccusker.com

Sunset
by G. Allen Wilbanks

The child's cry woke him from deep sleep. The dark elf cracked a bleary eye and peered toward the opening of his cave. The sun still illuminated the landscape and, while the crying human was tempting, the risk of daylight touching his skin was too great to risk leaving his den. Creatures such as he had their limits.

The elf closed his eyes and returned to slumber.

Later, the child's cry roused him yet again. As before, he peeked through sleep-heavy lids, but now discovered only darkness at the mouth of his cave.

Ahhh, he thought. *This changes things entirely.*

G. Allen Wilbanks is a member of the Horror Writers Association (HWA) and has published over 50 short stories in various magazines and on-line venues. He is the author of two short story collections, and the novel, When Darkness Comes.
Website: www.gallenwilbanks.com
Blog: DeepDarkThoughts.com

Reflection
by Kyle Harrison

Mirrors always look scariest in the dark.

They say if you want to see your past, that you can approach a mirror from behind with another smaller mirror. If you hold it up just right, you can peer inside the glassy reflection and discover what you are made of.

I've had nightmares lately, memories of something taking me by force in the night. I figured if I asked the mirror for answers, maybe it would make me sleep better.

I needed to know, what was happening to me.

But my surprise came when I found nothing at all staring back.

***Kyle Harrison** is a successfully published short story horror novelist and has been in over 6 anthologies and managed 3 anthologies himself. He has also been a project manager for Kickstarters and served as a mentor for other aspiring writers.*

A Late Night Hunt
by Stuart Conover

A howl broke through the air and Joseph started running.

He knew the sound of wolves.

This wasn't it.

He had never heard this before.

Primal fear kicked in.

Joseph knew he was not the hunter tonight.

He was half a mile in from the cabin he'd built years ago.

At full sprint it should take five minutes to get there.

In three Joseph could see the cabin.

He was going to make it!

As Joseph neared the clearing the wind was knocked out of him.

He tasted dirt and turned over just as fangs and white fur closed in.

Stuart Conover is a father, husband, rescue dog owner, published author, blogger, journalist, horror enthusiast, comic book geek, science fiction junkie, and IT professional. With all of that to cram in daily, we have no idea if or when he sleeps or how he gets writing done! (We suspect it has to do with having evil clones.) Stuart is a Chicago native and runs the author resource Horror Tree.

Cannibal Nurse
by Rowanne S. Carberry

Finally finished stripping the flesh off the joint of meat, Maggie turns the oven to 180, grabs the salt and pepper and starts to season the joint.

She drizzles on some oil, places it in a roasting dish and waits for the oven to heat up.

Tidying up she throws the toes into a bag and looks at the passed out man. She's cauterised the wound just below his knee, put him on IV antibiotics and painkillers but he still hasn't come round.

Hearing the oven ping, Maggie puts in the leg and thinks about which bit she'll cook next.

Rowanne S. Carberry was born in England in 1990, where she stills lives now with her cat Wolverine. Rowanne has always loved writing, and her first poem was published at the age of 15, but her ambition has always been to help people. Rowanne studied at the University of Sunderland where she completed combined honours of Psychology with Drama. Rowanne writes to offer others an escape. Although Rowanne writes in varied genres each story or poem she writes will often have a darkness to it, which helped coin her brand, Poisoned Quill Writing – Wicked words from a poisoned quill.
Facebook: PoisonedQuillWriting
Instagram: @poisoned_quill_writing

Candle Man
by Beth W. Patterson

Boogeyman? Well, you're close. Not boogey but bougie, which means "candle."

There's nothing to fear from a little flame, child. I thought you were afraid of the dark, but it seems my appearance frightens you more. I may look fearsome with my seven-foot-tall frame and sharp teeth, but I am a simple candle maker. My candlesticks are made of tallow, which comes from fat.

You're such a plump, healthy little boy. It's even more fortunate that you raided the cookie jar. Your mother called you naughty, but I think you're perfect. Let me pinch you.

You'll shine ever so brightly.

Beth W. Patterson was a full-time musician for over two decades before diving into the world of writing, a process she describes as "fleeing the circus to join the zoo". She is the author of the books Mongrels and Misfits, and The Wild Harmonic, and a contributing writer to twenty anthologies. Patterson has performed in eighteen countries, expanding her perspective as she goes. Her playing appears on over a hundred and sixty albums, soundtracks, videos, commercials, and voice-overs (including seven solo albums of her own). She lives in New Orleans, Louisiana with her husband Josh Paxton, jazz pianist extraordinaire.
Website: www.bethpattersonmusic.com
Facebook: bethodist

The Taste of Salt and Vengeance
by Aiki Flinthart

Becalmed, the trawler rests on infinity. Inky glass reflects the glittering milk wash overhead. We lean on the gunwale, coal-glowing cigarettes in hand, and suck salt-air smoke.

"They say things live in these seas," Josh says. "Angry things. We do bring up some weird shit."

"These the same people who say global warming's not real, Cap'n?" I ask.

He hawks; spits into the water. "Reckon we're killing the ocean?"

"Would you stop fishing, if we are?"

Josh shrugs. "Nope. Gotta eat."

"That's what I thought." I flute a warbling whistle.

A tentacle thicker than my body slaps onto the deck.

Aiki Flinthart has had short stories shortlisted in the Aurealis awards and top-8 listed in the USA Writers of the Future competition, as well as published in various anthologies and e-mags. She has 11 published spec fic novels and has edited 2 short story anthologies. She regularly gives workshops on writing fight scenes at conventions. Lives in Brisbane. Does martial arts, archery, knife throwing and lute-playing.
Website: www.aikiflinthart.com

Shadows
by Jensen Reed

Following my class of six-year-olds outside, faint screams drew my attention. *No…it's too early!* I looked at the sun, still firmly in the sky. *They can't come out until dark!*

"Ms. Holly?" a girl whimpered nearby. Shadows all around us began to lengthen and distort, and the children's screams filled my ears.

I stepped back inside and screamed, "Inside, NOW!"

They ran but not fast enough. The shadows reached and tangible claws raked against flesh, eliciting ear-splitting cries of pain.

"NO!" I stared in horror as the shadows enveloped torn bodies, which disappeared as if they were never even there.

Jensen Reed is a multi-published short story author, lead admin for Writing Bad, and mama to two boys. She dabbles in reading and writing genres but particularly enjoys feeding characters to zombies and making readers cry. Find her book links, flash fiction, and connect with her on her website. Website: authorjensenreed.wordpress.com

Camping Gone Wrong
by Alanna Robertson-Webb

How do you explain the sight of a creature like Nessie battling a creature like the Jersey Devil?

You can't.

I quickly discovered that, if you do try to, no one believes you. They'll call you crazy, or a liar, but that's what happened to me last summer. I was camping by the shore of Lackawanna Lake, and my tent catching on fire woke me.

I don't know if Nessie or Jersey won, since the lake monster dragged the hoofed thing into the water. Blood bubbled to the surface, and I left everything behind as I ran for my life.

Alanna Robertson-Webb is a sales support member by day, and a writer and editor by night. She loves VT, and lives in NY. She has been writing since she was five years old, and writing well since she was seventeen years old. She lives with a fiance and a cat, both of whom take up most of her bed space. She loves to L.A.R.P., and one day she aspired to write a horrifyingly fantastic novel. Her short horror stories have been published before, but she still enjoys remaining mysterious.
Reddit: MythologyLovesHorror

Choices
by Joel R. Hunt

Mark awoke to a row of glistening fangs.

"Another year gone…" hissed the beast, "Another chance to save your wretched hide."

"You know what my answer will be," Mark said, avoiding its gaze.

The beast shook its long snout.

"You must see them. You must choose."

As it spoke, an image of the beast's potential victim appeared. Not a stranger this year, but a friend. Sasha. Mark's dearest love.

It was an easy choice.

"Take me," Mark said, "Let her live."

The beast chuckled.

"That's convenient," it said.

"What do you mean?"

"Because earlier tonight, she chose you as well."

Joel R. Hunt is a writer from the UK who dabbles in the darker aspects of life, particularly through horror, science fiction and the supernatural. He has been published here and there (though likely nowhere you've heard of) and hopes to have released his first anthology of short stories later this year.
Twitter: @JoelRHunt1
Reddit: JRHEvilInc

Learning Curve
by Glenn R. Wilson

Billy never got it. Why? No one knew. He'd moved into the complex a month ago. Everyone wondered why all of his neighbours got sick, then bedridden, weaker, and died within two days. One after another. While, in fact, Billy seemed to grow larger and stronger throughout.

So, they called me.

It took as long as takes for me to tie my shoelaces to figure it out. So, I did what any good alien hunter would do: I blasted him.

They'll never learn how to identify a soul-sucking, parasitical vampire from the Cygnus solar system.

I call it job security.

Glenn R. Wilson has come full circle. Making a point to mature, like fine wine, before diving head-first into his long list of writing projects, he's approaching them with a plan. That strategy is to build with one brick at a time. He's accumulated a few bricks already and is adding more. Over time, with persistence and determination, he'll have a home. But for now, a solid foundation is the goal. Please, enjoy the process with him.

Last Call
by J.D. Bell

He sat eyeing the woman behind the bar. "Hey, babe, I'll have another." She poured him a whiskey. "What time do you get off, sugar?"

"Too late for you," she said.

"Come on. Don't be shy. I don't bite." he said.

She grinned. "What if I do?" she said.

"Sounds like fun," he laughed.

When he regained consciousness, he found himself strapped to a table. She wore blue latex gloves.

"This will be a night to remember. Time to have some fun," she said with a smile. The glint of the knife shined like a precious diamond in the light.

J.D. Bell *is an award-winning, internationally published, author of flash fiction and short stories. He recently retired from the world of writing advertising copy and is now enjoying the universe of creative fiction.*
Facebook: jim.writes.stories
Twitter: @JimBell58

It Came in Silence
by Gabriella Balcom

"Miserable buggers," Johnny groused at the mosquitoes droning around him. But then the pests vanished. The street lights went off, too. Shrugging, he walked down the road.

Something bit his neck, although he hadn't heard anything. He turned around, gasped, and stumbled backward.

An insect the size of a large dog hovered in the air, looking like a cross between a mosquito and wasp. Silently zooming forward, it grabbed Johnny and flew off.

Johnny yelled and flailed around but couldn't get loose. The creature jabbed him, and he felt his life draining away. Soon his body was a bloodless husk.

Gabriella Balcom lives in Texas with her family, loves reading and writing, and thinks she was born with a book in her hands. She works in a mental health field, and writes fantasy, horror/thriller, romance, children's stories, and sci-fi. She likes travelling, music, good shows, photography, history, interesting tales, and animals. Gabriella says she's a sucker for a great story and loves forests, mountains, and back roads which might lead who knows where. She has a weakness for lasagne, garlic bread, tacos, cheese, and chocolate, but not necessarily in that order.
Facebook: GabriellaBalcom.lonestarauthor

Legend
by Umair Mirxa

Lancelot felt the breaking of every bone in his body as he transformed into a werewolf. The full moon reached its apex, and he howled in ecstasy as he began to run. He had scouted the tiny hamlet for days and camped in the nearby forest the last three nights. Now, it was time to hunt.

Dawn came, and Lancelot returned to his human form. His victims lay strewn around him, most mangled beyond recognition. He walked away with a smile, licking his bloody lips. Word of his deeds would spread, and before anyone knew it, he would be legend.

Umair Mirxa lives in Karachi, Pakistan. His first published story, 'Awareness', appeared on Spillwords Press. He has also had stories accepted for anthologies from Zombie Pirate Publishing, Blood Song Books, Fantasia Divinity Magazine and Publishing, and Iron Faerie Publishing. He is a massive J.R.R. Tolkien fan, and loves everything to do with fantasy and mythology. He enjoys football, history, music, movies, TV shows, and comic books, and wishes with all his heart that dragons were real.
Website: www.umairmirxa.com
Facebook: UMirxa12

What Goes on Inside Her Head?
by Aiki Flinthart

She lies waiting, perfect. Her glassy eyes gaze at the bewebbed ceiling. Her hands are cold and smooth. Skin gleaming-pale, porcelain-pink.

When it's done will she understand? Will the world understand? Will I be despised? Lauded? The last line is written. Ready. But I hesitate and, instead, stroke her glossy black hair. Candlelight flickers, giving an illusion of movement.

Firming resolve, I open her skull, thrust the paper in, and say the spell.

She jerks and blinks. Her lips part.

No. This is wrong, this playing God.

I reach for her head.

Her hand grips mine. Snaps bones. I scream.

Aiki Flinthart *has had short stories shortlisted in the Aurealis awards and top-8 listed in the USA Writers of the Future competition, as well as published in various anthologies and e-mags. She has 11 published spec fic novels and has edited 2 short story anthologies. She regularly gives workshops on writing fight scenes at conventions. Lives in Brisbane. Does martial arts, archery, knife throwing and lute-playing.*
Website: www.aikiflinthart.com

Neighbourhood watch
by Crystal L. Kirkham

Marjorie was the neighbourhood watch—that was the joke. She stuck her nose in everyone's business.

When Dave moved into town, she did her usual spying, but he remained a mystery. Desperate to know more, she snuck into his yard that night and peaked in through a window.

She screamed when she saw him shed his skin. His red eyes met hers, but she couldn't move. Couldn't run as he came over and opened the window.

"Hello," he said, showing fearsome teeth. "I've been expecting you."

She sheds her skin at night now and, soon, all of the town would.

Crystal L. Kirkham resides in a small hamlet west of Red Deer, Alberta. She's an avid outdoors person, unrepentant coffee addict, part-time foodie, servant to a wonderful feline, and companion to two delightfully hilarious canines. She will neither confirm nor deny the rumours regarding the heart in a jar on her desk and the bottle of reader's tears right next to it. Her paranormal urban fantasy series, Saints and Sinners, is available on Amazon and her YA Fantasy, Feathers and Fae will be released October 11, 2019, from Kyanite Publishing.
Website: www.crystallkirkham.com

Demon's Breath
by Martin Eastland

Vicky carefully negotiated the dark, mist-enshrouded alleyway, her knuckles white in fear of what lay in wait in there. The full moon—leering…mocking…inviting, even—looked upon her with malicious indifference as the wind blew through the alley, causing craft to prosper in its wake. Bottles rolled along the gutters; pizza boxes careening off sleeping derelicts in the corners; and the eerie silence of inevitability descended upon her. A mist began to form behind her, getting thicker by the moment, and her grip intensified. Vicky could feel its eyes burning into her, and she slowly turned to face it.

Game over!

*Born in Glasgow, Scotland, **Martin Eastland** began his writing career at the age of 12, his only outlet allowing him to escape a less than harmonious childhood. Almost 30 years later, he has gone from strength to strength as a writer, expanding into new areas, but remaining loyal to his preferred genres of horror, and the suspense-thriller. He enjoys mainly short stories and flash fiction as he views it as being beneficial for his future development as an author. He is happily married with four children, and lives with his wife in Shropshire, England.*
Facebook: Martin-Eastland-245154596385827

Cave Dweller
by Eddie D. Moore

Matt made a shushing gesture and motioned Kalie to come closer to the edge. She kept one hand on the wall of the cave as she stepped forward to see Matt's promised surprise. The roiling mass of intertwined tentacles below didn't react to their lights.

Kalie whispered, "What is that thing?"

A long slender tentacle slowly reached up, and Kalie took a step back. Matt rested a hand on her shoulder, shook his head, and whispered, "Don't run. It will chase the sound."

Fear filled Kalie's voice. "Why did you bring me here?"

Matt answered, "Because she's hungry," and pushed.

Eddie D. Moore travels hundreds of hours a year, and he fills that time by listening to audiobooks. When he isn't playing with his grandchildren, he writes his own stories. You can find a list of his publications on his blog or by visiting his Amazon Author Page. While you're there, be sure to pick up a copy of his mini-anthology Misfits & Oddities.
Website: eddiedmoore.wordpress.com
Amazon: amazon.com/author/eddiedmoore

Spider Alert
by Cecelia Hopkins-Drewer

I always wondered why many monsters in movies looked like giant spiders, but never wanted to find the answer. However, my research as a biologist took me into the rainforests of far north Australia.

I heard a whistling noise and ought to have remembered some spiders rub their legs together to produce sound. I walked forward and found myself snagged in a huge web.

I activated my phone camera and began uploading the footage, even as the female spider approached. It bit me on the neck, and even paralyzed, I could feel it carrying me back to feed its young.

Cecelia Hopkins-Drewer is a speculative fiction writer, poet and scholar, who lives in Adelaide, South Australia. She has also written a Masters paper on H.P. Lovecraft, and a teenage vampire series that commences with "Mystic Evermore". Her science fiction poetry has been published in "The Mentor" a fanzine edited by Ron Clarke.
Amazon: amazon.com/Cecelia-Hopkins-Drewer/e/B071G968NM

Babes in the Swamp
by Beth W. Patterson

Don't say I didn't warn you, *chèr*. You go into the swamp at night, you're gonna see the *feu-follet*. Those *Américaines* call them "will o' the wisp," but we Cajuns know they're the spirits of unbaptised babies. People say that they'll lead you to treasure hidden by the pirate Jean Lafitte, but that ain't true. Believe me, I've tried.

They look so pretty at first, beckoning and playful. But as you get closer, they're like little white doll faces with empty eye sockets. And before long, you'll be lost in the bayou.

Now ask me how I lost my leg.

Beth W. Patterson was a full-time musician for over two decades before diving into the world of writing, a process she describes as "fleeing the circus to join the zoo". She is the author of the books Mongrels and Misfits, and The Wild Harmonic, and a contributing writer to twenty anthologies. Patterson has performed in eighteen countries, expanding her perspective as she goes. Her playing appears on over a hundred and sixty albums, soundtracks, videos, commercials, and voice-overs (including seven solo albums of her own). She lives in New Orleans, Louisiana with her husband Josh Paxton, jazz pianist extraordinaire.
Website: www.bethpattersonmusic.com
Facebook: bethodist

Wolf
by Sinister Sweetheart

The wolf is going to eat me, it's caught my scent and slowed.

The wolf is going to eat me. Our date; my husband never showed.

The wolf is going to eat me, the moon's full and bright.

The wolf is going to eat me, teeth glistening in moonlight.

The wolf is going to eat me, with breath muggy and thick.

The wolf is going to eat me, it pins my foot...I try to kick.

The wolf is going to eat me, that is no surprise.

The wolf is going to eat me, and he has my husband's eyes.

Since **Sinister Sweetheart** made her first post to a popular Internet forum, she's taken the horror community by storm. Her ability to create, terrify, and drive home her stories is insurmountable. Sinister Sweetheart's published works can be found in multiple anthologies for all to read, but be forewarned, if you do... you may want to call your therapist after, her stories are terrifying, disturbing and devilishly unsettling. She is not only a fright visually, but also has a creepy tentacle in horror podcasting as well. Sinister Sweetheart writes, voice acts and is the media director of the Scarecrow Tales podcast.
Website: Sinistersweetheart.wixsite.com/sinistersweetheart
Facebook: NMBrownStories

Dapper Dan
by Shelly Jarvis

I call the kids around the fire and in hushed tones recite, "Tonight I speak of days gone dark, a man transformed in this here park; his name is Dapper Dan."

The younger kids squirm, the older ones roll their eyes. Little brats. I continue, "His hands are claws, his teeth are long, he'll slice you, dice you, right or wrong; his name is Dapper Dan."

I whisper, "He kills the little camper boys, and makes their insides into toys…"

I pause for effect.

From the woods, a low growl, then a gravelly voice says, "My name is Dapper Dan."

Shelly Jarvis *is a speculative fiction author from West Virginia, US. She found a life-long love of sci-fi and fantasy in the 3rd grade when she found Madeleine L'Engle's "A Wrinkle in Time." Shelly is an avid reader, a Whovian, the ideal viewer of dog rescue videos, and undoubtedly Ravenclaw. She currently has two YA sci-fi books available for purchase on Amazon.*
Website: www.ShellyJarvis.com

A Cornfield of Blood
by Nerisha Kemraj

Jake shifted the tractor into gear—nothing worked.

Great.

Stuck in this stupid cornfield, miles away from home.

"Stupid piece of junk!" He kicked the monster wheel, in frustration, but an angry snarl quashed his pain.

"Who's there?"

Nothing.

Lifting the bonnet to check the engine, there it was again.

Glowing red eyes stared back from under the tractor-hood. The creature growled, baring incisive fangs. Jake backed away, tripping over a rock.

The beast struck, his long tail dangled Jake in the air. Horror-struck, Jake screamed as razor-like talons pierced into him. A cornfield of blood.

*Multi-genre (short-fiction) author, and poet, **Nerisha Kemraj**, resides in South Africa with her husband and two, mischievous daughters. She has work traditionally published/accepted in 30 publications, thus far, both print and online. She holds a BA in Communication Science from UNISA and is currently busy with a Post-Graduate Certificate in Education.*
Facebook: Nerishakemrajwriter

Mistress Moon
by Pamela Jeffs

Some of the others call her Mother Moon, but to me she is The Mistress.

And one so cruel.

I stand in the darkness, hidden behind the line of trees that back onto the house where once I lived. Windows, squares of warm light against the darkness, reveal to me the details of my old life. My wife—how tired and weary she looks! My children—crying for their father. I want to go to them, to comfort them. But I cannot. A wolf lurks beneath my skin. And in moments, when The Mistress emerges, the beast will claw free.

Pamela Jeffs is a speculative fiction author living in Queensland, Australia with her husband and two daughters. She is a member of the Queensland Writers' Centre and has had numerous short fiction pieces published in recent national and international anthologies. In 2017 and again in 2018, Pamela was nominated for an Australian Aurealis Award in the category of 'Best Science Fiction Short Story'. Her debut collection titled 'Red Hour and Other Strange Tales' was released in March 2018.
Website: www.pamelajeffs.com
Facebook: pamelajeffsauthor

Doppelganger
by Sinister Sweetheart

I awake to a sickening sound coming from the baby monitor. The squelching grows louder every step closer to my infant's room. My older son Nolan isn't in his bed.

He must've been in baby Logan's room. I couldn't scold him after he'd disappeared briefly earlier that day. I was too thankful to have him back with me.

The scent of copper's overwhelming as I enter Logan's room. Nolan's bent over his crib; he shakes violently as he tears his brother apart with his teeth.

What had come home with me wasn't my son, my son's still very far away.

*Since **Sinister Sweetheart** made her first post to a popular Internet forum, she's taken the horror community by storm. Her ability to create, terrify, and drive home her stories is insurmountable. Sinister Sweetheart's published works can be found in multiple anthologies for all to read, but be forewarned, if you do... you may want to call your therapist after, her stories are terrifying, disturbing and devilishly unsettling. She is not only a fright visually, but also has a creepy tentacle in horror podcasting as well. Sinister Sweetheart writes, voice acts and is the media director of the Scarecrow Tales podcast.*
Website: Sinistersweetheart.wixsite.com/sinistersweetheart
Facebook: NMBrownStories

Children of the Night
by Kevin Hopson

Unease crept over Steffon as he stood on the hilltop overlooking the once bustling town.

"It's nothing but a ghost town now," a voice said, causing Steffon to flinch. "My apologies for startling you. I'm Elgar. I used to live there."

"What happened?"

"When young children began disappearing at night, no one wanted to stay."

Steffon pondered. "An aswang?"

"A what?"

"A shape-shifting predator, but it's only a myth."

"Have you seen one before?"

A shiver escaped Steffon as he met Elgar's gaze. His reflection was upside-down in the man's eyes. Steffon swallowed, barely mustering a response. "Not until now."

*Prior to hitting the fiction scene in 2009, **Kevin Hopson** was a freelance writer for several years, covering everything from finance to sports. His debut work, World of Ash, was released by MuseItUp Publishing in the fall of 2010. Since then, Kevin has released over a dozen books through MuseItUp, and he has also been published in various magazines and anthology books. Kevin's writing covers many genres, including dark fiction and horror, science fiction and fantasy, and crime fiction.*
Website: www.kmhopson.com

The Monster's Lover
by Joel R. Hunt

She towered over the two humans—her captive and her lover—as she clutched her fierce snout in spade-like paws. At her feet, the captive groaned and struggled against the rope that bound them down.

"I can't…" she growled.

"You know how the curse works," replied her lover, "If you don't consume human flesh tonight, you'll die."

He reached out to caress her claws, but she pulled away.

"I can't kill someone," she said, "I may be an abomination, but I'm not a monster!"

He nodded, pulled out a knife and pressed it to the captive's throat.

"Well, I am."

Joel R. Hunt is a writer from the UK who dabbles in the darker aspects of life, particularly through horror, science fiction and the supernatural. He has been published here and there (though likely nowhere you've heard of) and hopes to have released his first anthology of short stories later this year.
Twitter: @JoelRHunt1
Reddit: JRHEvilInc

Curfew Keeper
by Dawn DeBraal

Herman Chatlers' face was horribly disfigured in the same fire that destroyed his mind. Cigarette smoking kids, breaking their curfew, started the house fire that nearly took Herman's life.

Now, he spends his evenings hunting children.

They were fair game if they didn't go home when the streetlights came on. At nightfall, Herman followed the children, scaring them by popping out from the bushes, singing out their names as he spied on them in play. The children would scream, running away, begging to be let into their homes. Herman became known by those who feared him most as the bogeyman.

Dawn DeBraal lives in rural Wisconsin with her husband, two rat terriers, and a cat. She successfully raised two children (meaning they didn't return to the nest!) After many years serving the government at the Federal and County level, she recently retired. Having extra time on her hands she started to write after a paralyzed vocal cord took her ability to speak for two months. Not finding her voice, she discovered that her love of telling a good story could be written. Her works have been published in Palm-sized press, Spillwords, Mercurial Stories, Potato Soup Journal, and Blood Song Books.

Bedtime
by Donald Jacob Uitvlugt

When she's six, she's oh so good. She brushes her teeth. She says her prayers. Checks under the bed. And makes sure her toes are tucked in tight.

The checking goes first. She's no longer a child. She doesn't believe in fairy tales. There's school and shopping and boys. Her cell phone alone hardly leaves time to brush her teeth. Once in the morning's enough.

Next to last go the prayers.

All grown up, she comes home drunk. She strips off shoes and socks and clothes and falls into bed.

And from under her bed, the monster licks her foot.

First appeared in 100 Horrors, edited by Kevin G. Bufton, 2012

***Donald Jacob Uitvlugt** lives on neither coast of the United States, but mostly in a haunted memory palace of his own design. His short fiction has appeared in numerous print and online venues, including Cirsova Magazine and the Flame Tree Press anthology Murder Mayhem. He works primarily in speculative fiction, though he loves blending and stretching genres. He strives to write what he calls "haiku fiction," stories that are small in scale but big in impact. Website: haikufiction.blogspot.com Twitter: @haikufictiondju*

Chasing Legends
by Eddie D. Moore

The tour group turned a corner, and Sam waited for the last person to pass from sight before slipping away. He found the stairway marked for authorised personnel only and ducked under the chain.

The air chilled as Sam descended, and goosebumps shook him. Legend claimed that the original owner was locked in a coffin alive and left in the lowest chamber of the castle after two local teenagers vanished.

When he reached the bottom, his flashlight spotlighted the expected coffin, but the chains were on the floor and the lid was open. Teeth flashed, and the flashlight winked out.

Eddie D. Moore travels hundreds of hours a year, and he fills that time by listening to audiobooks. When he isn't playing with his grandchildren, he writes his own stories. You can find a list of his publications on his blog or by visiting his Amazon Author Page. While you're there, be sure to pick up a copy of his mini-anthology Misfits & Oddities.
Website: eddiedmoore.wordpress.com
Amazon: amazon.com/author/eddiedmoore

Karma
by J.M. Ames

Carrie paid little attention to the dense fog that rolled into the bay and slowly enveloped the distant Golden Gate Bridge; she was focused on tying his weights to the maroon-stained rolled carpet alongside her. She paused to catch her breath, and glanced at Alcatraz, ensuring the tourists and guards had left for the day. She slid beside her newly wrapped gift to the sea, careful not to tip over the dinghy named *Karma*, and rolled that bastard's corpse into the murky depths. The fog swallowed *Karma* whole, as the leviathan's massive jaws arose from below and did the same.

J.M. Ames is an award-winning multi-genre speculative fiction author native to Southern California. He has multiple short story publications dating back to 2016. One thing holds true throughout all of his stories - you can Expect the Unexpected. When not working his day job or enjoying his fatherly adventures, he writes short stories and novels, including an upcoming series.
Website: jm-ames.com/contact-jm

Funhouse Monsters
by Gregg Cunningham

We followed the excited crowd into the funhouse, full of anticipation. The Halloween flier promised it to be the best horror house we'd ever seen.

We doubted that.

Inside, couples shrieked and giggled as the staff dressed in bloody clown costumes jump-scared punters from the shadows, but we just shook our heads in disappointment.

"Amateurs," Jack said, pulling the long machete from his pants.

I nodded, pulling the rubber masks from my pocket, and stepped into a side room with Jack.

"Grab the next couple that pass."

It turned out to be quite the horror house after all.

Who knew!

Gregg Cunningham 48, short story writer who has had to pick up his game since stumbling into facebook writer's groups. He has stories published by 559 Publishing in in 13 Bites volume 3,4,5, Plan 9 from Outer space, Other Realms, Heard It on The Radio, 559 Ways to Die, short stories publishing by Zombie Pirate Publishing in Relationship add Vice, Full Metal Horror, Phuket Tattoo, World War four and Flash Fiction Addiction (flash) with Zombie Pirate Publishing, and also in Daastan Magazine Chapter 11 and Brian,Rich and the Wardrobe.
Amazon: www.amazon.com/-/e/B016OTHX0K

Mourning Girl
by Ximena Escobar

Blood poured like soul. Like girl fading in wet stone. In mud. Where childhood happened but I can't relive the memories, staring into the non-reflection of my face. That dreadful garden is my face.

Will I be this emptiness forever?

Sun like paint flashes on the leaf. Mother sinks her brush under the tree as remnant of girl absorbs 'til the last spark—sharp like the fangs; his painful fangs tearing mother's canvas; drowning in red, my cadmium yellow hair cascading down my scathed knee.

It doesn't hurt.

I can't see girl, but I imagine my tongue licking the blood.

Ximena Escobar is an emerging author of literary fiction and poetry. Originally from Chile, she is the author of a translation into Spanish of the Broadway Musical "The Wizard of Oz", and of an original adaptation of the same, "Navidad en Oz". Clarendon House Publications published her first short story in the UK, "The Persistence of Memory", and Literally Stories her first online publication with "The Green Light". She has since had several acceptances from other publishers and is working very hard exploring new exciting avenues in her writing.
She lives in Nottingham with her family.
Facebook: Ximenautora

The Piper's Song
by Jodi Jensen

"I'm hungry, Mama."

"I know, baby." Mina ladled soup into a bowl as the Pied Piper's song filled the air outside. She nodded at the poisoned dish. "Eat every bite."

The music grew louder, the pallid-faced child, antsy.

"Quickly now." Mina held the bowl while her daughter slurped the last few drops. The front door crashed open and she froze as the Pied Piper filled the doorway.

He watched the little girl slump over the table and gasp her final breaths. He stepped aside to reveal dozens of glossy-eyed children, bloody weapons in hand. "And they say I'm the monster."

Jodi Jensen grew up moving from California, to Massachusetts, and a few other places in between, before finally settling in Utah at the ripe old age of nine. The nomadic life fed her sense of adventure as a child and the wanderlust continues to this day. With a passion for old cemeteries, historical buildings and sweeping sagas of days gone by, it was only natural she'd dream of time traveling to all the places that sparked her imagination.

That Damned Cat
by Stephen Herczeg

When I head down the staircase, that damned cat springs out of nowhere and runs between my legs again.

He keeps tripping me up, like he wants to hurt me, but I've grown more careful. I keep an eye out. Pay attention.

But today I forgot. Something sprang between my feet. Down I went.

I bounced, I heard a crack. My neck's at a weird angle, and I can't feel my body.

There he is. No, wait.

Those teeth. Those claws. Those baleful eyes. That's not him. That's not even a cat.

It's getting dark. I hope someone comes soon.

Stephen Herczeg is an IT Geek based in Canberra Australia. He has been writing for over twenty years and has completed a couple of dodgy novels, sixteen feature length screenplays and numerous short stories and scripts. His horror work has featured in Sproutlings, Hells Bells, Below the Stairs, Trickster's Treats #1 and #2, Shades of Santa, Behind the Mask, Beyond the Infinite; The Body Horror Book, Anemone Enemy, Petrified Punks and Beginnings. He has also had numerous Sherlock Holmes stories published through the Belanger Books - Sherlock Holmes anthologies.

The Hag
by Dusty Davis

"Daddy!"

Ethan woke with a start to the sound of his son calling out for him. He jumped out of bed and rushed across the hall to find Johnny sound asleep in his bed.

Sweat trickled down his forehead despite the chill that crept up Ethan's spine. He spun around to face the open closet and saw it.

Her eyes peered out of the darkness, staring a hole through Ethan. He turned to grab Johnny from the bed, but he wasn't fast enough. The hag was on him. Claw-like fingers pierced his back. Ethan crumbled, as Johnny's eyes popped open.

Dusty Davis is an author of poetry and dark fiction living in East Liverpool, Ohio. He is a former professional wrestler and according to his wife, is obsessed with Batman. Amazon: www.amazon.com/author/dustydavis

The Tooth Fairy
by J. Farrington

"Mom! A tooth's fell out!"

"What? You can't be serious, why didn't you warn me? We could have prepared! We could have hidden you!" Knuckles white as she grips her daughter's shoulders.

"He's coming for me, isn't he?" she asked her mother.

"Yes, with his big yellow eyes, bag of bloodied teeth and pouch of gold. He's coming for your teeth, fallen out or not. Once he gets one, he will want them all," She replied.

Looking her daughter directly in the eyes, "This isn't to scare you…this is to prepare you!"

"What can I do? To stop him?"

"Nothing."

J. Farrington is an aspiring author from the West Midlands, UK. His genre of choice is horror; whether that be psychological, suspense, supernatural or straight up weird, he'll give it a shot! He has loved writing from a young age but has only publicly been spreading his darker thoughts and sinister imagination via social platforms since 2018. If you would like to view his previous work, or merely lurk in the shadows...watching, you can keep up to date with future projects by spirit board or alternatively, the following;
Twitter: @SurvivorTrench
Reddit: TrenchChronicles

The Skeletons Are Coming
by Jensen Reed

"The ske-le-tons are com-ing…"

I looked up from my book to glare at my little brother. He smirked, knowing the song affected me.

"They'll cre-ep in, to wear your skin, then you'll be one in the mor-ning."

"Stop!" Mom's yell filled the house. His grin disappeared, leaving him eerily expressionless. I tried to refocus on my book, but the cemetery was awakening. The house is locked. I closed my eyes and breathed. You're safe.

The telltale sound of the deadbolt unlocking sent a rush of horror through me. Danny stood in the open doorway and smiled.

"The ske-le-tons are com-ing…."

Jensen Reed is a multi-published short story author, lead admin for Writing Bad, and mama to two boys. She dabbles in reading and writing genres but particularly enjoys feeding characters to zombies and making readers cry. Find her book links, flash fiction, and connect with her on her website. Website: authorjensenreed.wordpress.com

Darkness Washed Ashore
by E.L. Giles

"I'm afraid, Mama."

The boat swayed, hit by restless waves.

"Everything's fine, son."

"Does it hurt, Mama?"

The mother clamped a hand around the wound, the rows of teeth perfectly stamped into her putrefying flesh, the fever debilitating, the memory of the dead thing sinking its vile mouth into her skin vivid.

She smiled.

For hours they were adrift, until the land where no dead could reach finally appeared, its shore bathed in the moonlight.

Its guardian rushed over, pulling the boat ashore.

She handed him her frightened son.

"Be a good boy, okay?"

Her heart heavy, she left him.

E.L. Giles is a dreamer, passionate about art, a restless worker and a bit of a weird human. He started his artistic journey as a music composer until the need to put his thoughts and stories down on paper grew too strong for him to resist it any longer. He lives in the French Province of Quebec, Canada, with his girlfriend and two boys.
Facebook: elgilesauthor
Website: www.elgilesauthor.com

The Penanggal
by Patrick Winters

"Hurry!" Amina pleaded through her contractions. "It's still following!"

Ashraf glanced back, seeing their pursuer's strange silhouette against the moon. The sight forced his foot to the floor, and their car zoomed through the Titiwangsa Range.

"Aaaaaaaaagh!"

Ashraf glanced back again—and crashed their car right into a tree.

The hood crumpled; the front window shattered. Ashraf's head hit the wheel and he went still.

Amina trembled in the backseat, calling for her husband and unable to hold back anymore.

The Penanggal came floating in through the ruined windshield. And when Amina's baby came crying into life, the creature smiled.

Patrick Winters is a graduate of Illinois College in Jacksonville, IL, where he earned a Bachelor of Arts degree in English Literature and Creative Writing and achieved membership into Sigma Tau Delta, an international English honors society. Winters is now a proud member of the Horror Writers Association, and his work has been published in the likes of Sanitarium Magazine, Deadman's Tome, Trysts of Fate, and other such titles. A full list of his previous publications may be found at his author's site. Website: wintersauthor.azurewebsites.net/Publications/List

Something Follows
by Jefferson Retallack

Australia. Shipwrecked. They chose me to scout inland.

Why did I leave England for such uncertainty?

At least the April heat here is sweet, like Kent in August, but only by the coast. Beyond, away from the South Pacific, the temperature becomes feverish.

Something follows, perpetually in my umbra. Tricks play at my periphery.

Like me, my tracker is foreign to this place. A stowaway, like me.

It, or the wind, whisper my mother's name, *Elanora*, signalling that dropsy has claimed her now.

This wendigo must shadow me as punishment for abandoning my family. Death, now, preferable to its bedevilment.

Jefferson Retallack is an Australian writer of speculative fiction. He is based in Adelaide. His work draws influence from linguistic science fiction, the new weird and Australia's big things. Outside of the literary world, he skateboards on the weekends and spends afternoons on the beach with his partner, their son, and their Pomeranian, Tofu.
Website: jwretallack.wordpress.com
Twitter: @JWRetallack

The Bunyip
by Jefferson Retallack

Day two. The ocean is but a memory. I should have found a river before trekking this far inland.

The stink of the Wendigo plagues me, reeking of matted fur, too thick for the Australian sun, burned sour.

I pray for rain. Am I yet to see a single cloud?

At last, water.

Odd. I approach the creek, but my stalker keeps its distance.

I drink my fill and fill my flasks.

Something massive lurches out from the water. I'm terrified, cowering. I fail to act.

Above my own pong, the sour smell returns.

Scratching.

A thud.

A splash.

Silence.

Jefferson Retallack is an Australian writer of speculative fiction. He is based in Adelaide. His work draws influence from linguistic science fiction, the new weird and Australia's big things. Outside of the literary world, he skateboards on the weekends and spends afternoons on the beach with his partner, their son, and their Pomeranian, Tofu.
Website: jwretallack.wordpress.com
Twitter: @JWRetallack

The Shadows We Cast
by Jefferson Retallack

Day three. My hunger grows fervent.

Darkness approaches. I enjoy my first Australian breeze since washing ashore.

I find a corpse, long dead. It is vaguely human in anatomy, but thin and elongated beyond reason.

Continuing, the scorched stench of the Wendigo declines somewhat, perhaps lingering to feast on dead Mimis.

Night arrives. With it, lights. Distant, they dance upon the earth. I give chase.

Min Mins. They waltz around me. As they circle, I cast long shadows and glimpse—and know—the thing that has stalked me: The Black Shuck.

Why it never attacks me, I do not know.

Jefferson Retallack is an Australian writer of speculative fiction. He is based in Adelaide. His work draws influence from linguistic science fiction, the new weird and Australia's big things. Outside of the literary world, he skateboards on the weekends and spends afternoons on the beach with his partner, their son, and their Pomeranian, Tofu.
Website: jwretallack.wordpress.com
Twitter: @JWRetallack

Death Nears Twofold
by Jefferson Retallack

Day Four. Death nears twofold.

The Black Shuck pursues, persistence hunting me across the desert, and I am waterless.

Is it too late to backtrack to the now dried-up creek?

My best option at this point—however grim—might be to trap the dog, drain it of its blood. The longer I wait, the less hydrated both of us will become.

Near midnight, it makes the first move.

I try to flee, but my exhausted feet fail. The Shuck pins my shoulders, looming.

The last thing I know is meaty paws, and the smell of scorched dirt beneath its tread.

Jefferson Retallack is an Australian writer of speculative fiction. He is based in Adelaide. His work draws influence from linguistic science fiction, the new weird and Australia's big things. Outside of the literary world, he skateboards on the weekends and spends afternoons on the beach with his partner, their son, and their Pomeranian, Tofu.
Website: jwretallack.wordpress.com
Twitter: @JWRetallack

Not All of Me Dies in the Desert, But Enough
by Jefferson Retallack

Day Five. Dark cockatoos screech across the full moon.

The Black Shuck—hunting me, England to Australia—restrains me, fiery paws singeing my torso.

Suddenly, it cools and calms. The massive dog frees me as two ethereal figures—one man, one hound—drift down from the moon.

Paralysed, the spirits circle us. Mine advances until within me.

We are one, Mopaditis says.

My soul floats away with Mopaditis to the moon.

The spirit hound attempts the same, but the spiritless Shuck cannot be fed upon.

A husk, I am now tedious to the Shuck.

Former prey, I am truly alone.

Jefferson Retallack is an Australian writer of speculative fiction. He is based in Adelaide. His work draws influence from linguistic science fiction, the new weird and Australia's big things. Outside of the literary world, he skateboards on the weekends and spends afternoons on the beach with his partner, their son, and their Pomeranian, Tofu.
Website: jwretallack.wordpress.com
Twitter: @JWRetallack

Leave None Alive
by Neen Cohen

"Hello, my monster." Feral eyes belied the sweet trill of her voice.

The wolf stalked toward her, the height of his back almost reaching her full stature. She rested her body against his soft pelt.

"You didn't leave any breathing I hope!" She absently stroked her own hand, bright teeth marks glistened in the light of her first full moon.

His low growl the only reply.

She nodded and undid the tie around her neck. A breeze picked up the red cloak with hood as she watched her hands change. Paws hit the ground and she howled at the moon.

Neen Cohen lives in Brisbane with her partner, son and fur babies. She is a writer of LGBTQI, dark fantasy and horror short stories and has a Bachelor of Creative Industries from QUT. She can often be found writing while sitting against a tombstone or tree in any number of graveyards.
Facebook: Neen-Cohen-Author-424700821629629
Website: wordbubblessite.wordpress.com

Sweet Liquid
by A.R. Johnston

That sweet liquid of red was like gold that needed to flow down the throat. That succulent taste of skin beneath the tongue. Shivers down the spine at the pop the skin makes when biting down. There was nothing like it in the world.

He danced her close. Holding her tight, her sigh of contentment as she rested her head on his shoulder. He grinned, kissing her neck. She made a sound of assent. He gave the spot above her pulse a kiss and a teasing lick. He struck, his teeth sinking in, he pulled deep on her hot blood.

A.R. Johnston is a small-town girl from Nova Scotia, Canada. Her style of writing is considered Urban Fantasy. Her first major publication is part of an anthology called First Love and she has several more titles lined up. She is a lover of coffee, good tv shows, horror flicks, and reader of books. She pretends to be a writer when real life doesn't get in the way. Pesky full-time job and adulting!

Happy Hour
by Raven Corinn Carluk

Bowie's was a popular hangout for Hunters. A place to let their guard down without fear of civvies freaking out or monsters getting past Bowie's wards.

Yet every Hunter was taken by surprise when eight rougarou charged through the door.

Snarls filled the air. Wolfmen leapt on the nearest Hunters, tearing them apart. Blood flew, and a few screams sounded.

Guns fired. The rougarou continued their attack with one fewer. Hunters drew silver knives, moving into melee against them.

It ended with blood everywhere. Eight dead rougarou. Twenty-six dead hunters, five more dying. Merely a skirmish in the endless war.

Raven Corinn Carluk is an indie author of dark fantasy and paranormal romance.
Website: RavenCorinnCarluk.Blogspot.Com

Rest Your Weary Head
by Jonathan Inbody

His headache was getting worse. That new pillow wasn't helping at all, and as he scarfed down a microwave burrito he wondered if he would get any sleep tonight. He got back in bed and laid down but didn't feel the strings of living fabric dig into the back of his head and wriggle into the folds of his brain. The living pillow quickly put him to sleep with more poison, then fed him a nice dream to distract him as it continued eating. It wished the man hadn't just eaten that midnight snack; it was bad for the digestion.

Jonathan Inbody is a filmmaker, author, and podcaster from Buffalo, New York. He enjoys B-movies, pen and paper RPGs, and New Wave Science Fiction novels. His short story "Dying Feels Like Slowly Sinking" is due to be published in the anthology Deteriorate from Whimsically Dark Publishing. Jon can be heard every other week on his improvisational movie pitch podcast X Meets Y.
Website: xmeetsy.libsyn.com

Room with a Disturbing View
by John H. Dromey

"Good grief, Anna, your flat is tiny. Where do you sleep?"

"In a Murphy bed."

"Can you show it to me?"

"Sure. I'll get my sleeping mask."

"Why?"

"I don't want to risk seeing the monster under the bed as it clings to the underside of the springs. Promise me you'll shut your eyes."

Emily crossed her fingers. "Okay."

Anna opened the wall panels and lowered the bed. "What do you think?"

No reply.

She turned around, raised the lower corner of the mask, and peeked at her friend.

Emily was in a catatonic state. Her hair had turned white.

John H. Dromey was born in northeast Missouri, USA. He enjoys reading—mysteries in particular—and writing in a variety of genres. He's had short fiction published in Alfred Hitchcock's Mystery Magazine, Martian Magazine, Stupefying Stories Showcase, Thriller Magazine, Unfit Magazine, and elsewhere, as well as in a number of anthologies, including Chilling Horror Short Stories (Flame Tree Publishing, 2015).

The Coyote
by Alanna Robertson-Webb

I live in an isolated region of New Mexico, and in the last week five of my cattle have been slaughtered. At first, I thought it was a cougar, or even a human, but the bite marks seem to be a weird mashup of canine and human, which makes no sense.

The only thing different around here lately is a lone coyote. I've seen it slinking around the cow fence, and it seems to be deformed. Its legs are too long, and its howl sounds more like a human screaming.

Could that weird coyote be responsible for killing my cows?

Alanna Robertson-Webb is a sales support member by day, and a writer and editor by night. She loves VT, and lives in NY. She has been writing since she was five years old, and writing well since she was seventeen years old. She lives with a fiance and a cat, both of whom take up most of her bed space. She loves to L.A.R.P., and one day she aspired to write a horrifyingly fantastic novel. Her short horror stories have been published before, but she still enjoys remaining mysterious.
Reddit: MythologyLovesHorror

Blind Date
by Henry Herz

"Lunch has been lovely," she said. "I'd heard that first dates can be quite awkward. But mine have gone particularly badly. I may be no Helen of Troy, but you would think I'm a monster the way your ill-mannered predecessors just clammed up. I had to carry both sides of the conversation."

"Well, I find your wit charming," he replied, raising a hand to call for the check.

"I've been admiring your sunglasses. But why are you wearing them in a restaurant?" she asked.

"Oh, I thought you knew. I'm blind," he replied.

"Ah, that explains a lot," said Medusa.

Henry Herz edited the dark fantasy anthology, BEYOND THE PALE, featuring stories by Saladin Ahmed, Peter Beagle, Heather Brewer, Jim Butcher, Rachel Caine, Kami Garcia, Nancy Holder, and Jane Yolen. His horror story, Gluttony, will appear in the anthology, CLASSICS REMIXED. He authored the children's books: MONSTER GOOSE NURSERY RHYMES, WHEN YOU GIVE AN IMP A PENNY, MABEL & THE QUEEN OF DREAMS, LITTLE RED CUTTLEFISH, CAP'N REX & HIS CLEVER CREW, HOW THE SQUID GOT TWO LONG ARMS, ALICE'S MAGIC GARDEN, GOOD EGG AND BAD APPLE, TWO PIRATES + ONE ROBOT, THE MAGIC SPATULA, and I AM SMOKE.
Website: www.henryherz.com

Salvation
by Matthew M. Montelione

The dishevelled doctor guzzled the liquid. "This is it, Dave! Our salvation is at hand!" he yelled as he tugged on his long dark hair.

Dave recoiled.

"What's wrong?" the doctor asked as he cocked his neck.

"Last time you tried controlling him, he fought back."

The doctor snorted and banged a pipe against the floor. "That was a mistake!"

It was too late. The doctor vomited. Foul smelling gas left him as he convulsed. He let out a garbled roar as he transformed into a seventeen-foot tall orange gorilla. Vomit dripped from his lips.

He crushed Dave to bits.

Matthew M. Montelione *is a horror writer born and raised on Long Island in New York. His stories have been published in Quoth the Raven: A Contemporary Reimagining of the Works of Edgar Allan Poe, Thuggish Itch: Devilish, MONSTERS: A Horror Microfiction Anthology, Eerie Christmas, and other titles. Matthew is also an American Revolution historian who focuses on the local experiences of Loyalists on Long Island. His work on the subject has been published in Long Island History Journal and Journal of the American Revolution. Matthew lives with his wife in New York.*
Website: maybeevils.com
Twitter: @maybeevils

The Smiling Visitor
by Kaustubh Nadkarni

Every night it peeks through the window and gingerly enters my bedroom. Two smouldering red eyes slice through the darkness. It vigorously nods its head and waddles towards my bed. My muscles are frozen as it casually sits on my chest. A wide smile reveals bare gums, and a gust of putrid breath hits my face. It sits for hours together, staring blankly at me. Finally, it waddles back to the window.

My psychiatrist says it's sleep paralysis, but those red eyes haunt my soul. Tonight, it enters again. But this time, I look down from the ceiling and smile.

Kaustubh Nadkarni is an Indian medical practitioner. He loves to unwind, with a mystery novel and a cup of steaming hot chai. Exploring hidden worlds within pages makes him happy. He dabbles in drabbles, short stories, and poetry. When he's not scribbling words, Kaustubh enjoys football and photography. His works have appeared in: Dark Drabbles 4, Sea Glass Hearts and Elemental Drabbles Vol. 1.
Twitter: @kaustofsuccess
Instagram: @kaustofsuccess

The Manor
by Jem McCusker

High atop the gateposts, they crouched with fangs of rock, horns and sharp wicked tails. The grandfather clock of Fenwick Manor struck the hour as the moon burst free from the shadow of clouds.

"Ouch! Christopher, that's my head."

"Shut it, Jamesy." Christopher clambered on the boy's shoulders, pulling himself up onto the gate post.

"I want to come this time…please?"

"Next time." Christopher removed his lad cap, placing it on the gargoyle's head before grinning smugly at his brother.

Christopher reached for his hat and the trapped creature broke free clasping his hand.

"Dinner is served!" The gargoyle lunged

Jem McCusker is a middle grade fiction author, living near Brisbane with her two sons and husband. Her first book Stone Guardians the Rise of Eden was released in 2018 and she is working on the sequel. She is releasing a Novella for the Four Quills writing group, A Storm of Wind and Rain series in July, 2019. She longs to be a full-time author, won't wear yellow and loves rabbits. Follow Jem on Twitter, Facebook and Instagram. Details on her website.
Website: www.jemmccusker.com

Instinct
by Rich Rurshell

Everybody started running, so I did too. I didn't bother looking back, I just sprinted to keep up with them. I didn't want to be left behind.

One guy ran into an alleyway, so I followed him. It was a dead end. He turned and screamed as I caught up with him. Whatever it was chasing us must have followed me.

It was only when I bit into his neck and tore out his throat that I realised what everyone was running from.

I did not want this, yet I have vague recollections of this kind of thing happening before.

Rich Rurshell is a short story writer from Suffolk, England. Rich writes Horror, Sci-Fi, and Fantasy, and his stories can be found in various short story anthologies and magazines. Most recently, his story "Subject: Galilee" was published in World War Four from Zombie Pirate Publishing, and "Life Choices" was published in Salty Tales from Stormy Island Publishing. When Rich is not writing stories, he likes to write and perform music.
Facebook: richrurshellauthor

Here, Boy
by Ximena Escobar

"Here, boy," he said.

He didn't need to give him any meat. Just the flesh of kindness—a pat on the head, a snap of his fingers—and the dog followed.

He let him tie the noose around his neck. He'd seen other dogs walking along parks with swings and families; ties around their necks too. So he let him, watching as he looped the rope to the back of the car. Then the boy got in and the engine purred.

The dirt road scraped his skin as he bounced, dragged and breaking.

Waiting like vomit on the train track.

Ximena Escobar is an emerging author of literary fiction and poetry. Originally from Chile, she is the author of a translation into Spanish of the Broadway Musical "The Wizard of Oz", and of an original adaptation of the same, "Navidad en Oz". Clarendon House Publications published her first short story in the UK, "The Persistence of Memory", and Literally Stories her first online publication with "The Green Light". She has since had several acceptances from other publishers and is working very hard exploring new exciting avenues in her writing.
She lives in Nottingham with her family.
Facebook: Ximenautora

A Message Untold
by Crystal L. Kirkham

Razor sharp claws dripped with blood as the beast screamed with rage. Viscera coated the walls and bodies littered the room, left where they had fallen.

We observed and made notes from the safety of another room. No one wanted to be the next victim of this nightmare from an unknown land.

"Look over there." Anson pointed at what the creature had scratched into the walls. "That looks organised, like it's trying to write something."

"No, it's not intelligent, it's a monster." I didn't tell them that I could read what was written. It was the language of my home.

Crystal L. Kirkham resides in a small hamlet west of Red Deer, Alberta. She's an avid outdoors person, unrepentant coffee addict, part-time foodie, servant to a wonderful feline, and companion to two delightfully hilarious canines. She will neither confirm nor deny the rumours regarding the heart in a jar on her desk and the bottle of reader's tears right next to it. Her paranormal urban fantasy series, Saints and Sinners, is available on Amazon and her YA Fantasy, Feathers and Fae will be released October 11, 2019, from Kyanite Publishing.
Website: www.crystallkirkham.com

Vector of Madness
by J.D. Bell

The spores had travelled far, floating free on gentle breezes, searching for a new host. A lone grey wolf served their purpose. They bored into the animal's skull, burrowing deep into its brain. They fed on nervous tissue, transforming the wolf from a focused hunter into a manic killer.

The wolf ran wild, frenzied and uncontrolled. The beast raged with an overwhelming lust to kill driven by the spores. The deed was merciless as the wolf tore ribbons of flesh and pieces of limb from the unsuspecting hiker. As the hiker lay dying, the spores bored deep into his brain.

J.D. Bell *is an award-winning, internationally published, author of flash fiction and short stories. He recently retired from the world of writing advertising copy and is now enjoying the universe of creative fiction.*
Facebook: jim.writes.stories
Twitter: @JimBell58

Under the Bed
by Melissa Neubert

Her parents promised her there weren't monsters under the bed. She knew they lied. She heard them in the deepest dark of the night, crawling around, scratching. Waiting. She put her headphones in to drown out the noise. She closed her eyes hoping for sleep. Sleep, without monsters invading her dreams, which rarely happened.

When she woke up, there was a green slimy creature sleeping beside her. She froze, her heart raced. She moved slowly hoping for escape. She almost made it when she felt a clammy claw encircle her arm, stopping her in her tracks. Her parents definitely lied.

Melissa Neubert was born in the Pacific Northwest and currently lives in Illinois with her husband, three children and two dogs. Melissa has been a daycare provider, veterinary assistant, teacher/library aide, and administrative assistant. Melissa travels extensively both domestically and internationally where she finds inspiration for her writing in beautiful and unique locations. When she is not writing she enjoys music, reading, concert and wildlife photography, football and camping. Although Melissa has been writing since grade school, she has only recently begun pursuing the craft seriously. She writes mostly in the genres of Suspense/Thriller and Adult Paranormal Romance.

The Transaction
by D.M. Burdett

The wind brought his scent, heady and beautiful, and it wrapped around me like a heavy blanket, muffling the street sounds and enveloping me in its embrace. I tried to ignore the mounting pressure within, but my skin crawled with wonting. I stepped out of the alley as he approached.

"How much?" he asked before following me back into the darkness.

His hands ran over my body as he thrust, and I pulled him close, my lips grazing his neck. As he reached his climax, I sank my teeth and gulped from the pumping vein, my own desire finally satiated.

D.M. Burdett initially roamed as an army brat, but now lives in Australia where she spends her days avoiding drop bears and killer spiders. She has published a Sci-Fi series, has short stories in various anthologies, and has published two children's series. She is currently working on the first book in a dystopian series.
Website: www.dmburdett.com
Facebook: DMBurdett

The Forest
by Gabriella Balcom

"I could lose my rig," Murray argued.

"So, don't get caught," Rodney retorted. "This saves my company a ton of money and I pay you well, so get the job done."

Hours later, Murray stopped in a remote, forest location, and drained toxic sludge from his truck into the small cave he'd discovered years earlier.

***

A few years later

The hiker didn't know something watched him from behind.

Creeping toward him, the misshapen, two-headed alligator looked to his right, left, and then attacked. Terrified screams rang out, then stopped.

Word soon spread about something killing people in the National Forest.

Gabriella Balcom *lives in Texas with her family, loves reading and writing, and thinks she was born with a book in her hands. She works in a mental health field, and writes fantasy, horror/thriller, romance, children's stories, and sci-fi. She likes travelling, music, good shows, photography, history, interesting tales, and animals. Gabriella says she's a sucker for a great story and loves forests, mountains, and back roads which might lead who knows where. She has a weakness for lasagne, garlic bread, tacos, cheese, and chocolate, but not necessarily in that order.*
Facebook: GabriellaBalcom.lonestarauthor

Nectar
by Umair Mirxa

Niobe drew Argus closer to her breast, trying desperately to shield him from the serpentine monster.

"Give the child to me," hissed the monster as it approached. "Surrender it, and I shall let you live."

"Why would you come after a son of Zeus, Lamia? He loved you. He helped you," pleaded Niobe. "Please, I beg of you. Let Argus live."

"*Helped* me? He *should* have saved my children. Now, I shall drink the nectar from the veins of his offspring and be truly immortal."

Hermes found Niobe hours later, her eyes gouged out. There was no sign of Argus.

Umair Mirxa lives in Karachi, Pakistan. His first published story, 'Awareness', appeared on Spillwords Press. He has also had stories accepted for anthologies from Zombie Pirate Publishing, Blood Song Books, Fantasia Divinity Magazine and Publishing, and Iron Faerie Publishing. He is a massive J.R.R. Tolkien fan, and loves everything to do with fantasy and mythology. He enjoys football, history, music, movies, TV shows, and comic books, and wishes with all his heart that dragons were real.
Website: www.umairmirxa.com
Facebook: UMirxa12

Rorrim
by Alanna Robertson-Webb

Do you ever get the feeling that, when you look in the mirror, your reflection doesn't quite follow you? Sometimes it seems to lag by just a fraction of a second, and it's so subtle that it's almost impossible to perceive it.

I noticed.

When I raise my hand to wave it takes just a moment longer for my reflection to wave back. When I laugh, my reflection's mouth seems to open just a little wider than mine.

Last night was the worst though. While I was crying, my reflection was grinning back at me, and its eyes were pitch-black.

Alanna Robertson-Webb is a sales support member by day, and a writer and editor by night. She loves VT, and lives in NY. She has been writing since she was five years old, and writing well since she was seventeen years old. She lives with a fiance and a cat, both of whom take up most of her bed space. She loves to L.A.R.P., and one day she aspired to write a horrifyingly fantastic novel. Her short horror stories have been published before, but she still enjoys remaining mysterious.
Reddit: MythologyLovesHorror

The Monsters Under the Bed
by Gregg Cunningham

I can still hear them calling to me from the darkness below, each one louder than the previous snarling demand. Even from within their cardboard box I hear them laugh as I bury my head into my pillow pleading for them to stop, pleading to them for mercy.

But they show none. Why should they? They showed none to my father before they made him take his own life. They showed none to my mother before she took her life. And now they want me.

Every ignored, red-lined, final demand from the evil providers want their unpaid pound of flesh.

Gregg Cunningham *48, short story writer who has had to pick up his game since stumbling into facebook writer's groups. He has stories published by 559 Publishing in in 13 Bites volume 3,4,5, Plan 9 from Outer space, Other Realms, Heard It on The Radio, 559 Ways to Die, short stories publishing by Zombie Pirate Publishing in Relationship add Vice, Full Metal Horror, Phuket Tattoo, World War four and Flash Fiction Addiction (flash) with Zombie Pirate Publishing, and also in Daastan Magazine Chapter 11 and Brian,Rich and the Wardrobe.*
Amazon: www.amazon.com/-/e/B016OTHX0K

Suits
by Lynne Lumsden Green

I find wearing a suit is like wearing a mask. Every morning, when I put my suit on, I feel it harder to breathe, my movements are restricted, I am not myself anymore. When I look in the mirror, I see a bland, normal human face. I dress in my work clothes and toddle off to catch the bus.

Is my true form so repulsive? I'd be more graceful if I could use all my arms and legs. I'd have better vision if I could use all my eyes. Why can't I trust human beings to love me for myself?

Lynne Lumsden Green has twin bachelor's degrees in both Science and the Arts, giving her the balance between rationality and creativity. She spent fifteen years as the Science Queen for HarperCollins Voyager Online and has written science articles for other online magazines. Currently, she captains the Writing Race for the Australian Writers Marketplace on Facebook. She has had speculative fiction flash fiction and short stories published in anthologies and websites.
Website: cogpunksteamscribe.wordpress.com

Greedy What?
by R.G. Halstead

The young man looked baffled. "But...greedy plumbers gotta work and eat, too, Mama."

"Uh, huh. Greedy monster plumbers who quote three times higher than the other plumbers that was here. Three times! He's gonna be back here in a half hour to fix our toilet. I phoned the greedy monster again."

"But, Mama, as soon as he lifts up the toilet seat there...he'll be grabbed and dragged down into the plumbing pipes by the monster that Papa created. It's still down there, Mama. It'll rip and tear away at that plumber. He'll—"

"Uh, huh. Monsters gotta eat, too."

R.G. Halstead, a 63-year-old, takes to writing late in his life. Influences? Those old Alfred Hitchcock Mystery Magazines from the late 1950s and the 1960s with the great twisty endings. Love them.

Trapped
by Joshua D. Taylor

When I woke up trapped underneath my overturned car on a remote stretch of highway, I thought I would die of internal bleeding. Now I'm not so sure. Hungry eyes watch me from inside a nearby drain pipe. The sun is starting to go down. The darker it gets, the brighter and closer the glowing eyes get. I can hear its ragged breaths and the scratching of claws. There is a pungent smell like rotting meat and musk wafting from the pipe.

It's getting cold. Maybe I'll freeze to death. I hope it happens soon. The eyes are getting closer.

Joshua D. Taylor is an amateur writer who started writing a few years ago when he realised he was too old to play make-believe. He lives in southeastern Pennsylvania with his wife and a one-eared cat. He enjoys gardening, comic books, ska-punk music, Disney World, and travelling with his wife. Raised during weirdness that was the late 20th century Josh's eclectic interests produce eclectic works. He loves to mix-n-match things from different genres and stories elements to achieve a madcap hodgepodge of the truly unexpected. His short story 'the Obelisk' appears in Salty Tales by Stormy Island Publishing.
Facebook: authorjoshuadtaylor

Freedom
by Eddie D. Moore

Darrel found a cellar door under the old carpet in his bedroom. Five years of ownership and he had no idea that there was a cellar under the house. His excitement grew when he lifted the door and saw the steps leading down into the darkness.

Using the flashlight app on his phone, he began descending the stairs. The third step creaked and then suddenly snapped, sending Darrel tumbling to the bottom. Something moved in the shadows as he panned his light, making his heart pound in his chest.

A voice whispered, "Freedom," just before claws dug into his eyes.

Eddie D. Moore travels hundreds of hours a year, and he fills that time by listening to audiobooks. When he isn't playing with his grandchildren, he writes his own stories. You can find a list of his publications on his blog or by visiting his Amazon Author Page. While you're there, be sure to pick up a copy of his mini-anthology Misfits & Oddities.
Website: eddiedmoore.wordpress.com
Amazon: amazon.com/author/eddiedmoore

Takeover
by C.L. Williams

Teddy walked around holding his stomach as he writhed in pain. At first, people checked on him to see if he was ok, but when he told people something was inside him and taking over his body, they assumed he just wanted attention and walked away. The one day it happened, the truth came to light.

He falls down and a snake-like entity bursts out of his stomach, "I am Ekboc and I am now this human. You will forget all!" The snake then slides back into Teddy's body and continues living life as Teddy and none notice anything different.

C.L. Williams is an independent author from central Virginia. He has written eight poetry books, four novellas, one novel, and a contributor to multiple anthologies, with the most recent appearance being an all-ages anthology titled Temoli from Thazbook. His most recent poetry book, The Paradox Complex, features the poem "Sad Crying Clown" that is now a video on YouTube directed by Matthew Mark Hunter of MMH Productions. C.L. Williams is currently working on his first sci-fi book, an all-ages book titled Novo: Away from Earth. When not writing, C.L. Williams is reading and sharing the work of other independent authors. Facebook: writer434
Twitter: @writer_434

The Amateur and the Prince
by Hari Navarro

Roland Shunt loves three things; family, vampires and teeth. He believes the Twilight saga is under-appreciated genius. An obsession that leads him to become Wisborg County's pre-eminent orthodontist.

Roland is dragging Angela Grunes into a storm-drain, in his mouth a dental contraption of his own design—porcelain fangs, perfect fit for his foaming snarl.

Chomping her flesh. Calculation's off, can't open his jaw enough to latch on—slobbering her neck. Angela's forehead smashes, grin shattered, blood streams the incisor protruding his lip.

Scent of his cells waft the drain, drawn into ancient hungry lungs—behold the sanguisuge prince!

Hari Navarro has had work published at the very fine online flash fiction portal 365tomorrows.com, BREACH - a bi-monthly online zine for SF, horror and dark fantasy short fiction and AntipodeanSF - Australia's longest running online speculative fiction magazine. Hari was the Winner of the Australasian Horror Writers' Association [AHWA] Flash Fiction Award 2018 and has, also, succeeded in being a New Zealander who now lives in Northern Italy with no cats.
Facebook: HariDarkFiction
Twitter: @HariFiction

Of Demi Gods and Chimera
by Pamela Jeffs

The sun is high. Against its flaming disc, the silhouette of Pegasus cavorts. On his back rides Bellerophon, a demi-god whelp. The pair has come to kill me. Are they brave or stupid? I cannot decide.

I raise my lion head and roar my challenge. I breathe out my fiery breath and let my dragon-headed tail bare its teeth. I am the Chimera. I am a monster of immortal make and will not bow to any man, king, or godly hero that comes to claim my head for his trophy.

My attackers dip out of the sky.

I prepare myself.

Pamela Jeffs is a speculative fiction author living in Queensland, Australia with her husband and two daughters. She is a member of the Queensland Writers' Centre and has had numerous short fiction pieces published in recent national and international anthologies. In 2017 and again in 2018, Pamela was nominated for an Australian Aurealis Award in the category of 'Best Science Fiction Short Story'. Her debut collection titled 'Red Hour and Other Strange Tales' was released in March 2018.
Website: www.pamelajeffs.com
Facebook: pamelajeffsauthor

Dr Frankenstein's Monster Repurposed
by John H. Dromey

Disappointed by a lack of accolades in the scientific community for his ground-breaking achievements, and bone-weary of being accosted almost daily by angry villagers armed with pitchforks and flaming torches, Dr Frankenstein decided to relocate.

His promethean construct would make an ideal gladiator—taking on all opponents, man or beast—in a Roman Circus. Those exhibitions, alas, were long gone. Was there anything vaguely similar in the modern highly mechanised world?

Yes.

There was a way his creature could engage in wanton destruction while simultaneously savouring the adulation of adoring fans! Put him in a stadium in a Monster Truck.

John H. Dromey was born in northeast Missouri, USA. He enjoys reading—mysteries in particular—and writing in a variety of genres. He's had short fiction published in Alfred Hitchcock's Mystery Magazine, Martian Magazine, Stupefying Stories Showcase, Thriller Magazine, Unfit Magazine, and elsewhere, as well as in a number of anthologies, including Chilling Horror Short Stories (Flame Tree Publishing, 2015).

Night View
by Shawn M. Klimek

It had been a perfect day for a beach picnic, and several couples lingered to observe Nature's programmed double feature: a glorious sunset followed by a full moonrise. As the sea breeze quickened, Kim and Colin cuddled closer, neither initially noticing as not just one, but two full moons began to ascend. For several minutes of overheard "oohs" and "ahs" and chatter about whether the cause must be a trick of light or an orb-shaped cloud, romance trumped curiosity. It was the cries of terror that first made them look up. Beneath the giant eyes, a monstrous mouth had appeared.

Shawn M. Klimek is the middle child of seven creative siblings, a globetrotting, U.S. military spouse, an internationally best-selling short-story writer, a poet, and butler to a Maltese. Almost one hundred of his stories or poems have been published in digital magazines or anthologies, including BHP's Deep Space and the first six books in the Dark Drabbles series.
Website: jotinthedark.blogspot.com
Facebook: shawnmklimekauthor

The Brookville Baptist Church
by Brian Rosenberger

My family was Lutheran but went to the Baptist Church. It was convenient. Mom didn't drive. Dad drove off, never to return, shortly after I was born.

Church was never my thing. Boring. Sometimes we played basketball between preaching. I wish we went to some kind of snake-handling church. Would've been more interesting. That was then.

Now we huddle in the pews, the ones that are left, offering prayers to any God that will listen. The bats circle the rust-coloured sky. We call them bats but they have too many teeth. We call ourselves sinners. Or just unlucky. Yeah. Unlucky.

***Brian Rosenberger** lives in a cellar in Marietta, GA (USA) and writes by the light of captured fireflies. He is the author of As the Worms Turns and three poetry collections. He is also a featured contributor to the Pro-Wrestling literary collection, Three-Way Dance, available from Gimmick Press.*
Facebook: HeWhoSuffers

Thriving
by Rennie St. James

The mere whisper of the word monster commands fear and loathing. It conjures images; pitiful innocents brutalised by terrifying, bloodthirsty creatures of the night. The hunter and the hunted. Good versus evil. Life and death.

Not all monsters seek your destruction; some of us treasure your life. Breaking bones is easier than corrupting souls. It takes time for a demon to burrow inside the human heart and mind. But we can, and we do.

When you thrive, we thrive.

The next time you hear the word monster, look into the mirror. Pride goeth before a fall, my foolish human friend.

Rennie St. James shares several similarities with her fictional characters (heroes and villains alike) including a love of chocolate, horror movies, martial arts, history, yoga, and travel. She doesn't have a pet mountain lion but is proudly owned by three rescue kitties. They live in relative harmony in beautiful southwestern Virginia (United States). The first three books of Rennie's urban fantasy series, The Rahki Chronicles, are available now. A new series and several standalone stories are already in the works as future releases.
Website: writerRSJ.com

Her Brother
by Melissa Neubert

She always knew her brother was weird; he painted his room black, he had no friends. The books he read were creepy. She figured it was a phase he would outgrow. Besides, he's only ten. Most ten-year-old boys were pretty weird.

But the day she came home and found he had killed the cat she knew it wasn't a phase. Fresh blood dripped off his mouth as he devoured his pet. He looked up at her, his eyes glittered golden, there was no guilt, no regret, he smiled revealing his fangs. She had no doubt; her brother was a monster.

Melissa Neubert was born in the Pacific Northwest and currently lives in Illinois with her husband, three children and two dogs. Melissa has been a daycare provider, veterinary assistant, teacher/library aide, and administrative assistant. Melissa travels extensively both domestically and internationally where she finds inspiration for her writing in beautiful and unique locations. When she is not writing she enjoys music, reading, concert and wildlife photography, football and camping. Although Melissa has been writing since grade school, she has only recently begun pursuing the craft seriously. She writes mostly in the genres of Suspense/Thriller and Adult Paranormal Romance.

Oculus
by Umair Mirxa

Orithyia crouched in the tall grass and hefted her spear. Her consort moved beside her as the rest of her Amazons took position.

"Remember, my Queen," said Asteria. "Aim for the oculus. It is the only way to kill it."

"I know it well, love," said Orithyia.

The cyclops, when it came, lumbered through, dragging a gigantic mace along the ground. The Queen saw her moment, stood, and let her spear fly. A split second later, it had found its mark in the monster's single eye.

"Well, he will no longer trouble Themiscyra," said Orithyia, standing over the fallen cyclops.

Umair Mirxa lives in Karachi, Pakistan. His first published story, 'Awareness', appeared on Spillwords Press. He has also had stories accepted for anthologies from Zombie Pirate Publishing, Blood Song Books, Fantasia Divinity Magazine and Publishing, and Iron Faerie Publishing. He is a massive J.R.R. Tolkien fan, and loves everything to do with fantasy and mythology. He enjoys football, history, music, movies, TV shows, and comic books, and wishes with all his heart that dragons were real.
Website: www.umairmirxa.com
Facebook: UMirxa12

Art is in the Eye of the Beholder
by Aiki Flinthart

"You want to report a basilisk?" I stifled a laugh. Sighing, I logged the call. "Making a statue of your husband isn't a crime, ma'am, but I'll visit your neighbour." I hung up and grabbed my uniform jacket. Crazies, today.

A woman answered my knock. Thick blonde dreadlocks tied under a floppy hat. Mirrored glasses and a tie-dyed shirt. Hippie.

She smiled and pulled her shoulders back. "Well, hello."

"We've complaints about statues and a missing husband." I cleared my throat. "You don't have a…basilisk, do you?"

She lowered her glasses, showing eyes of milk. "Basilisk, no. Gorgon, yes."

Aiki Flinthart *has had short stories shortlisted in the Aurealis awards and top-8 listed in the USA Writers of the Future competition, as well as published in various anthologies and e-mags. She has 11 published spec fic novels and has edited 2 short story anthologies. She regularly gives workshops on writing fight scenes at conventions. Lives in Brisbane. Does martial arts, archery, knife throwing and lute-playing.*
Website: www.aikiflinthart.com

Feeding the Fish
by Vonnie Winslow Crist

Standing on the observation deck, Kelly tossed bread to catfish churning the water behind the reservoir's upper dam. She was mesmerised by their glazed eyes, thrashing tails, and hungry mouths.

The whiskered creatures were dark. Kelly spotted something paler. To get a better look, she crawled under safety chains, then climbed down steps until she was at water's edge.

Dozens of catfish gazed up at her as a whitish tentacle flew from the water, encircled her ankle, and yanked her in.

As the ancient evil drew her to its snapping beak, she struggled—but was devoured slowly, very slowly, nevertheless.

Vonnie Winslow Crist is author of The Enchanted Dagger, Owl Light, The Greener Forest, Murder on Marawa Prime, and other award-winning books. Her fiction is included in "Amazing Stories," "Cast of Wonders," "Outposts of Beyond," Killing It Softly 2, Defending the Future - Dogs of War, Midnight Masquerade, Chaos of Hard Clay, and elsewhere. A cloverhand who has found so many four-leafed clovers she keeps them in jars, Vonnie strives to celebrate the power of myth in her writing.
Website: www.vonniewinslowcrist.com

The Ghouls
by Stuart Conover

Decay filled his nostrils and Jason tensed.

One of them was close.

Early on many joked about the dead.

Zombies. Vampires.

But ghouls were what they were.

Something no longer human.

There was no drive to feed.

They just came back to kill.

And kill they did.

He avoided cities and graveyards like the plague.

Yet, one of them had found him.

Its shadow moved.

Quieter than it had any right to be.

Once it had been a woman.

Jason had to run.

Turning, he came face to face with a young girl.

What had once been a young girl.

Stuart Conover is a father, husband, rescue dog owner, published author, blogger, journalist, horror enthusiast, comic book geek, science fiction junkie, and IT professional. With all of that to cram in daily, we have no idea if or when he sleeps or how he gets writing done! (We suspect it has to do with having evil clones.) Stuart is a Chicago native and runs the author resource Horror Tree.

I See Dead Folks
by Gregg Cunningham

If I stare long enough and try not to blink, the shadows appear in the corner of my eyes. They are blurry to begin with, so I just stay still and watch them go about their daily business.

Sometimes I like to follow them, just to see what they do while they are walking in the park or sitting on a bench.

If I am quiet, I find that I can creep up on them as they take their selfies, scare the shit out of them when they see my ghostly white face staring back at them from their phones.

Gregg Cunningham 48, short story writer who has had to pick up his game since stumbling into facebook writer's groups. He has stories published by 559 Publishing in in 13 Bites volume 3,4,5, Plan 9 from Outer space, Other Realms, Heard It on The Radio, 559 Ways to Die, short stories publishing by Zombie Pirate Publishing in Relationship add Vice, Full Metal Horror, Phuket Tattoo, World War four and Flash Fiction Addiction (flash) with Zombie Pirate Publishing, and also in Daastan Magazine Chapter 11 and Brian,Rich and the Wardrobe.
Amazon: www.amazon.com/-/e/B016OTHX0K

Nectar
by Rich Rurshell

The fog had descended quickly, but not nearly as quickly as the beast that had created it. At first, we had no idea of its size. We just heard the buzzing overhead and the screams of those it was taking.

Then a vast shadow fell over us, and Katy was plucked from our group by long, grotesque limbs. We watched in horror as she was lifted towards a twitching proboscis. Her screaming ceased as it entered her skull. She disappeared into the fog.

A moment later, the shadow moved away, and a lifeless and empty Katy fell to the ground.

Rich Rurshell is a short story writer from Suffolk, England. Rich writes Horror, Sci-Fi, and Fantasy, and his stories can be found in various short story anthologies and magazines. Most recently, his story "Subject: Galilee" was published in World War Four from Zombie Pirate Publishing, and "Life Choices" was published in Salty Tales from Stormy Island Publishing. When Rich is not writing stories, he likes to write and perform music.
Facebook: richrurshellauthor

The Hunter
by Brian Rosenberger

He had killed animals on every continent, heard stories of giant wolves running wild in some forgotten village, but didn't believe until he saw the scars on a fellow hunter. He had survived the attack, sold all his guns, and now attended church dutifully in his wheelchair.

No wolves so far, but at least there was the whorehouse.

She was beautiful, if hirsute, and told him about the wolves. Extinct. But nature finds a way.

She mounted him. Her back arched unnaturally.

"Worth the trip," he thought when she suddenly yelled "Children."

No wolves, but their parasites. Nature adapted.

Were-fleas.

Brian Rosenberger lives in a cellar in Marietta, GA (USA) and writes by the light of captured fireflies. He is the author of As the Worms Turns and three poetry collections. He is also a featured contributor to the Pro-Wrestling literary collection, Three-Way Dance, available from Gimmick Press.
Facebook: HeWhoSuffers

Worse Than Scorned
by Kelly A. Harmon

"A woman aboard ship is bad luck," roared the captain. "Throw her overboard!"

"No! No—"

The sailors grabbed Marta and tied her legs together, wrapping the rope up around her shoulders so she couldn't swim.

"I curse you!" she yelled. "I'll return upon my death to haunt you all."

The seamen holding Marta balked, so the captain shoved her over.

Down, down, down she sank…until her legs fused together, and gills formed.

There, deep beneath the sea she met other women treated just the same.

"What do we do now?" Marta asked.

"We find a rocky cove and sing."

Kelly A. Harmon is an award-winning journalist and author, and a member of the Science Fiction & Fantasy Writers of America and Horror Writers of America. A Baltimore native, she writes the Charm City Darkness series. The fourth book in the series, In the Eye of the Beholder, is now available. Find her short fiction in many magazines and anthologies, including Occult Detective Quarterly; Terra! Tara! Terror! and Deep Cuts: Mayhem, Menace and Misery. Website: kellyaharmon.com Twitter: @kellyaharmon

It's Coming
by J. Farrington

If you receive this message, please, please keep moving…

The warnings from around the world were scattered…at first. But then all communications stopped. I just hope I have reached you in time. I don't know how long I have left; they're gaining on us quicker than we can run.

Do you hear it? That subtle humming noise, like a distant engine? If you live in the city you have no chance, you won't hear it coming. It's too late for you.

It blocks out the sun, a thousand mouths with rows upon rows of razor sharp teeth.

It's coming.

J. Farrington is an aspiring author from the West Midlands, UK. His genre of choice is horror; whether that be psychological, suspense, supernatural or straight up weird, he'll give it a shot! He has loved writing from a young age but has only publicly been spreading his darker thoughts and sinister imagination via social platforms since 2018. If you would like to view his previous work, or merely lurk in the shadows…watching, you can keep up to date with future projects by spirit board or alternatively, the following;
Twitter: @SurvivorTrench
Reddit: TrenchChronicles

A Longing for Snakes
by Shelly Jarvis

It slithers down the hall. Not like a snake, no; the thing twitches and jerks, contorts into strange shapes as it gets closer. I don't know what it is, but I can feel dread seeping through my skin as I watch.

It is made of darkness. Not just dark, or black, but void. It pulls at the dim hallway light, sucking it away until there is nothing. I can't see it, but I hear the slurp as it slides along the floor.

There is nowhere to run where it won't follow. It comes to pull the light out of me.

Shelly Jarvis is a speculative fiction author from West Virginia, US. She found a life-long love of sci-fi and fantasy in the 3rd grade when she found Madeleine L'Engle's "A Wrinkle in Time." Shelly is an avid reader, a Whovian, the ideal viewer of dog rescue videos, and undoubtedly Ravenclaw. She currently has two YA sci-fi books available for purchase on Amazon.
Website: www.ShellyJarvis.com

Matchwood
by Pamela Jeffs

The waves are wild. Sea foam washes the deck, pushed against the mast in cotton-like clusters by the wind. One wave crests higher than the rest. Thick and heavy it rolls by us, the indigo water shifting colour through to sickly yellow. Then I comprehend the truth. It's not water, but cephalopod flesh—even easier to recognise when the suckered underside slithers by.

"Thar' she is!" cries the barrelman from the crows nest. "The Kracken. She rides!"

My men are brave. Their pistols are held steady.

But even so, my ship splinters to matchwood when the first massive tentacle falls.

Pamela Jeffs is a speculative fiction author living in Queensland, Australia with her husband and two daughters. She is a member of the Queensland Writers' Centre and has had numerous short fiction pieces published in recent national and international anthologies. In 2017 and again in 2018, Pamela was nominated for an Australian Aurealis Award in the category of 'Best Science Fiction Short Story'. Her debut collection titled 'Red Hour and Other Strange Tales' was released in March 2018.
Website: www.pamelajeffs.com
Facebook: pamelajeffsauthor

Manchine
by Cecelia Hopkins-Drewer

Clunk knew that he was part man, part machine, but he refused to accept that he was not still human and longed to have a beer with his mates.

That evening, Clunk rebelliously rolled his way towards the hotel. His best friend saw Clunk and shouted for him to return to the garage. Clunk rolled forward. His mate slipped and went under the enormous machine body.

Clunk had been created after his body had been dismembered in an industrial accident. A sentient piece of mining equipment was immeasurably useful in remote and dangerous situations. Now the company would have two.

Cecelia Hopkins-Drewer is a speculative fiction writer, poet and scholar, who lives in Adelaide, South Australia. She has also written a Masters paper on H.P. Lovecraft, and a teenage vampire series that commences with "Mystic Evermore". Her science fiction poetry has been published in "The Mentor" a fanzine edited by Ron Clarke.
Amazon: amazon.com/Cecelia-Hopkins-Drewer/e/B071G968NM

Blackwood Lake
by Eddie D. Moore

Andrew placed a few branches on the fire and flipped the rifle's safety off. The light reflected off eyes in the water and under the brush of the opposite bank. He leaned his back against a large hardwood tree and waited.

Four people had vanished in the last month around Blackwood Lake, and Andrew was here to discover how. He smiled as a large set of eyes surfaced and slowly approached the bank.

Andrew attempted to lift his rifle and realised that he couldn't move. Roots tightened as a large mouth opened in the tree's trunk swallowing his muffled screams.

Eddie D. Moore travels hundreds of hours a year, and he fills that time by listening to audiobooks. When he isn't playing with his grandchildren, he writes his own stories. You can find a list of his publications on his blog or by visiting his Amazon Author Page. While you're there, be sure to pick up a copy of his mini-anthology Misfits & Oddities.
Website: eddiedmoore.wordpress.com
Amazon: amazon.com/author/eddiedmoore

And Then Daddy Was Gone
by Stephen Herczeg

He comes every night. Daddy leaves the night light on. It usually works.

But last night he just wouldn't go away. He's got braver.

I could see his claws reach out of the closet. They were long and sharp. I heard them scrape on the door as he dragged them back inside.

Then I heard the door creak open. I saw his shadow on the wall as he came into the room.

I screamed.

Daddy was there in a flash.

I pointed at the closet. Daddy smiled and poked his head inside.

And then Daddy was gone.

I screamed again.

Stephen Herczeg is an IT Geek based in Canberra Australia. He has been writing for over twenty years and has completed a couple of dodgy novels, sixteen feature length screenplays and numerous short stories and scripts. His horror work has featured in Sproutlings, Hells Bells, Below the Stairs, Trickster's Treats #1 and #2, Shades of Santa, Behind the Mask, Beyond the Infinite; The Body Horror Book, Anemone Enemy, Petrified Punks and Beginnings. He has also had numerous Sherlock Holmes stories published through the Belanger Books - Sherlock Holmes anthologies.

A Tequila Bottle
by Gabriella Balcom

"I said keep 'em coming!" Homer yelled. "So gimme another."

"No," the bartender replied. "You've already had a dozen beers and more than enough whiskey."

Grabbing an unopened bottle of tequila by its neck, Homer smashed the bottom against the bar and brandished the jagged end.

The bartender fled. Homer gasped when the worm in his bottle crawled out, grew larger, then slid up his arm. Despite the man's efforts to knock the ever-expanding creature off, it wrapped itself around his chest. Moving higher, it encircled his neck. He screamed, clawed at the thing, but it squeezed until he collapsed.

Gabriella Balcom lives in Texas with her family, loves reading and writing, and thinks she was born with a book in her hands. She works in a mental health field, and writes fantasy, horror/thriller, romance, children's stories, and sci-fi. She likes travelling, music, good shows, photography, history, interesting tales, and animals. Gabriella says she's a sucker for a great story and loves forests, mountains, and back roads which might lead who knows where. She has a weakness for lasagne, garlic bread, tacos, cheese, and chocolate, but not necessarily in that order.
Facebook: GabriellaBalcom.lonestarauthor

Kissed by a Kelpie
by Rowanne S. Carberry

A black mane of hair runs down her back, startling silver eyes are surrounded by thick black lashes. They're staring out at the man on the shore who's filled with indecision.

"The water's warm," she shouts.

He catches a glimpse of her flesh in the moonlight and makes up his mind. Clothes off in a flash, he jumps in the water and straight to her embrace.

She kisses him, and they fall under the waves.

She kisses him even as he struggles to breathe.

Drinking down the water flooding into his lungs she smiles as he takes his last breath.

Rowanne S. Carberry was born in England in 1990, where she stills lives now with her cat Wolverine. Rowanne has always loved writing, and her first poem was published at the age of 15, but her ambition has always been to help people. Rowanne studied at the University of Sunderland where she completed combined honours of Psychology with Drama. Rowanne writes to offer others an escape. Although Rowanne writes in varied genres each story or poem she writes will often have a darkness to it, which helped coin her brand, Poisoned Quill Writing – Wicked words from a poisoned quill.
Facebook: PoisonedQuillWriting
Instagram: @poisoned_quill_writing

Revenge
by K.T. Tate

Humans came, burning and burying us under their idea of progress. They called us monsters, demons. With faith and flame they fought, seeking our destruction.

But we are not so easily defined or defeated. Injured, we withdrew when they destroyed our shrines.

Now we watch and wait. Whispering in the darkness we pollute their sleep, like they polluted our land. We corrupt their children, filling them with old magic and curiosity. Time will be their downfall.

Soon their children will rise up, changed, hybrid. They will sing the rites that call us back. And on that day, we shall feast.

K.T. Tate lives in Cambridgeshire in the UK. She writes mainly weird fiction, cosmic horror and strange monster stories.
Website: eldritchhollow.wordpress.com
Tumblr: eldritch-hollow.tumblr.com

The Pale People
by Terry Miller

Rob sat in the chair, watching as the pale woman stripped the skin revealing the muscle beneath. Sara's flesh, meticulously removed, became a suit as the woman slowly stitched up the front, belly button to breasts.

She stood in front of a dusty mirror, smoothing down the sides like a woman in a wedding dress. Their bodies were similar, the measurements almost identical. She admired the craftwork of her stitches, like a corset perfectly laced.

The woman faced Rob, Sara's face sent chills down his spine. The wood floor creaked as a pale man stepped out of the dim corner.

Terry Miller is an author and 2017 Rhysling Award-nominated poet residing in Portsmouth, OH, USA. He has self-published a dark poetry collection on Amazon and one short story to date. His work has also appeared in Sanitarium, Devolution Z, Jitter Press, Poetry Quarterly, O Unholy Night in Deathlehem, and the 2017 Rhysling Anthology from the Science Fiction and Fantasy Poetry Association.
Facebook: tmiller2015

Locked Away
by Alexander Pyles

Leaving it imprisoned was a mistake. A dull continuous beat thumped through the house. An eternal drumming as certain and unceasing as my heartbeat. A deep elemental throb pulsing through my body.

It went on for days. Months. Years. My wife left, taking the children. The rhythm hounded me. I watched the basement door, exhale and inhale with each blow.

I needed to end it. I threw open the door and the pounding stopped. The sudden silence made me sway, losing my footing. I tumbled down into the dark, coming face to face with my corrupting shame, my own putrefaction.

Alexander Pyles resides in IL with his wife and children. He holds an MA in Philosophy and an MFA in Writing Popular Fiction. His short story chapbook titled, "Milo (01001101 01101001 01101100 01101111)," from Radix Media, is due out fall 2019. His other short fiction has appeared on 101fiction.org, River and South Review, and other venues. Website: www.pylesofbooks.com Twitter: @Pylesofbooks

Mouths to Feed
by Zoey Xolton

Breathless, Ruby waited. Seconds passed. Silence. The only sound, the thundering of her own heart. She counted to ten, cautiously opening the restroom door. The corridor was clear. She slipped out, quiet as a mouse. Like a shadow she slunk through the abandoned primary school. For two precious minutes she heard nothing. Blessed peace. Then, softly at first, she heard them. Moaning. Rasping. They called to her with their rotting maws. *Come play with us*, they sang. *Stay with us.* Rounding the corner, she froze. Vacant eyes and bloody smiles greeted her.

"Hello, children."

One-hundred hands reached to embrace her.

First published in *Trembling with Fear*, 2019

Zoey Xolton is an Australian Speculative Fiction writer, primarily of Dark Fantasy, Paranormal Romance and Horror. She is also a proud mother of two and is married to her soul mate. Outside of her family, writing is her greatest passion. She is especially fond of short fiction and is working on releasing her own themed collections in future.
Website: www.zoeyxolton.com

Savage Winter
by Brian Rosenberger

The bear had attacked three of Billy Two-Shadows' tribesmen. Among them, the chief's daughter. Billy had lived in exile for many moons. A message was sent. Billy understood. He tracked the bear for days. It was close. The smell in the frigid air—Death.

Before him, a black giant, its snout stained red by a dead elk. The beast weighed 200 pounds. Gaunt for such a creature. It had been a savage winter.

Arrows emerged from its shoulder. Billy wondered if it had encountered a werewolf before. Praying to the moon above, he growled it would never encounter another.

Brian Rosenberger lives in a cellar in Marietta, GA (USA) and writes by the light of captured fireflies. He is the author of As the Worms Turns and three poetry collections. He is also a featured contributor to the Pro-Wrestling literary collection, Three-Way Dance, available from Gimmick Press.
Facebook: HeWhoSuffers

All Guts, No Glory
by Beth W. Patterson

Not even a visit to the killing fields compared to the shrieks I heard that night.

My tuk-tuk driver had warned me about the malevolent spirits here in Cambodia. But after a long day of playing music for obnoxious expats, I zoned out.

The screams that tore me awake should have sent me anywhere but outside. What I saw almost didn't make sense: the head and torso of a woman flying through the air, trailing her heart, lungs, and intestines behind her.

The Khmers told me that she is an Ahp. If I'm lucky, the curse won't seize me too.

Beth W. Patterson was a full-time musician for over two decades before diving into the world of writing, a process she describes as "fleeing the circus to join the zoo". She is the author of the books Mongrels and Misfits, and The Wild Harmonic, and a contributing writer to twenty anthologies. Patterson has performed in eighteen countries, expanding her perspective as she goes. Her playing appears on over a hundred and sixty albums, soundtracks, videos, commercials, and voice-overs (including seven solo albums of her own). She lives in New Orleans, Louisiana with her husband Josh Paxton, jazz pianist extraordinaire.
Website: www.bethpattersonmusic.com
Facebook: bethodist

Burn Your Bridges
by Austin P. Sheehan

There is a darkness coming. The forest echoes with thunder, the air is thick with fear. There is pain ahead.

My heart races, but mind is calm and sure. This is what I have been waiting for; the night of thunder, the night of pain. My axe glints in the torchlight—it too has waited long.

Tasting the fear in the air, I drop the flaming torch onto the wooden bridge. The only way off this cursed island.

Axe in hand, I return to the village with a smile on my lips and a song of revenge in my heart.

Austin P. Sheehan is a writer of speculative fiction, a lover of language, literature and '90s TV. Armed with a psychology degree, he went into the world to study humanity, and now prefers the company of his wife and their greyhounds. He grew up in the valleys of Victoria's high country, and despite living in Melbourne, always feels at home amongst the mountains. You'll often find mountains in his stories, whether they're sci-fi, fantasy or alternative history.
Website: austinpsheehan.com
Twitter: @AustinPSheehan

Stolen
by Adam S. Furman

The noises begin the same as every other night: scratching, crashing, screeching. This time, I hear a muffled cry. It sets me upright and dashing out of my bedroom.

I follow the sound down the stairs, where a creature waits poised to leap. Standing waist high, it appears human, but it's a wretched thing.

Cradled in its arms is my son, fast asleep, unable to see the terror on my face. The imp's mouth curls into a grin. It turns and skips out the front door. I chase after it, but it's lost in the darkness with my little boy.

Adam S. Furman lives in rural Illinois with his family which includes a lot of kids (like...a lot). He generally writes science fiction.
Twitter: @AdamSFurman

Modern Dating
by J.M. Meyer

My date, Phil, walked through the door. He looked as he promised and smiled. So far so good. Our waitress, Tamara, scowled when she saw Phil, hiding behind his menu. I asked for martinis as she walked away, and Phil simultaneously ran in the opposite direction and out the door. Tamara set down the drinks with a folded note.

"Die—666."

Old, alone and poor after I pay for all these drinks, I thought.

Phil was back, car-crucifix in hand, running towards me yelling "No," as I gulped down the acid in my glass. Tamara was nowhere to be found.

J.M. Meyer is writer, artist and small business owner living in New York., where she received her master's degree from Teacher's College, Columbia University. Jacqueline loves the science fiction and horror genres. Reading Ray Bradbury was a mind-blowing experience for her in 8th grade. Alfred Hitchcock and Rod Serling were the horror heroes of her youth. Mercedes M. Yardley is her current horror writing hero. Jacqueline also enjoys the company of her husband Bruce and their three children, Julia, Emma and Lauren. Jacqueline's mantra: The only time it's too late to try something new is when you are dead.
Website: jmoranmeyer.net
Twitter: @moran_meyer

Fun House
by A.R. Johnston

They were supposed to bring joy, happiness, make you laugh until your stomach hurt, right? The makeup, funny shoes, crazy hair, silly walk. It was all just for fun wasn't it?

She choked on a breath as she tried not to scream. Tears streamed down her face as she watched in terror.

This clown was bubbly, bright, and joyous covered in gore and blood. The clown did a little dance as he made his way toward her. His makeup was streaked with arterial spray, his smile almost seemed demonic.

"What fun shall we have with you?" He giggled at her.

A.R. Johnston is a small-town girl from Nova Scotia, Canada. Her style of writing is considered Urban Fantasy. Her first major publication is part of an anthology called First Love and she has several more titles lined up. She is a lover of coffee, good tv shows, horror flicks, and reader of books. She pretends to be a writer when real life doesn't get in the way. Pesky full-time job and adulting!

The Limping Man
by C.L. Williams

Malcolm was enjoying a day at the park. Sitting outside and enjoying some food. While eating, an odorous, limping man makes his way towards Malcolm. "Can I help you?" Malcolm asks the limping man. Without saying a word, the limping man lunges his way to Malcolm and takes a bite out of Malcolm's face. Malcolm then gets on top of the limping man and punches his face. His hand now covered in blood and what looks like decayed skin, Malcolm makes his way to the bathroom to clean himself. Before he can get there, the urge for flesh takes over.

C.L. Williams is an independent author from central Virginia. He has written eight poetry books, four novellas, one novel, and a contributor to multiple anthologies, with the most recent appearance being an all-ages anthology titled Temoli from Thazbook. His most recent poetry book, The Paradox Complex, features the poem "Sad Crying Clown" that is now a video on YouTube directed by Matthew Mark Hunter of MMH Productions. C.L. Williams is currently working on his first sci-fi book, an all-ages book titled Novo: Away from Earth. When not writing, C.L. Williams is reading and sharing the work of other independent authors.
Facebook: writer434
Twitter: @writer_434

Evil Hides in the Multitude
by Carole de Monclin

At first, we barely paid them any mind. The creatures were few, small and innocuous looking. Nobody saw them as a threat.

But when we weren't looking, they thrived and multiplied beyond control. Eating everything in their path, they left the soil naked for the winds to feast on and precipitated the extinction of entire species. The damages their invasion caused will take centuries to heal.

Even if one's a drop in the ocean, I have my rifle aimed at the little bastard scampering across the Outback. Banner for a false innocence, its long ears and fluffy tail taunt me.

Carole de Monclin has lived in France and Australia, but for the moment the USA is home. She finds inspiration from her travels. She loves Science Fiction because it explores the human mind in a way no other genre can. Plus, who doesn't love spaceships and lasers? Her stories appear in the Exoplanet Magazine and Angels - A Dark Drabbles Anthology.
Website: CaroledeMonclin.com
Twitter: @CaroledeMonclin

Dandy Dogs
by Vonnie Winslow Crist

Walking home, Wilbur heard the distant cry of hounds. Slightly unnerved, he increased his pace. Still, the pack drew nearer.

Perhaps someone is hunting fox, he thought as he began to jog.

The melancholy baying grew louder.

Wilbur glanced behind, saw black hounds exhaling fire.

The devil's dandy dogs out to catch a soul, he thought. He ran as fast as he could.

The dogs yelped furiously, and a voice said, "Too late."

Wilbur tripped, fell to the ground. Gazing at the saucer-eyed, horned being reaching toward his chest he screamed for help.

The devil laughed, then took his soul.

Vonnie Winslow Crist is author of The Enchanted Dagger, Owl Light, The Greener Forest, Murder on Marawa Prime, and other award-winning books. Her fiction is included in "Amazing Stories," "Cast of Wonders," "Outposts of Beyond," Killing It Softly 2, Defending the Future - Dogs of War, Midnight Masquerade, Chaos of Hard Clay, and elsewhere. A cloverhand who has found so many four-leafed clovers she keeps them in jars, Vonnie strives to celebrate the power of myth in her writing.
Website: www.vonniewinslowcrist.com

Killers
by S. Gepp

They were after him. Already they'd struck true, and he was feeling the effects. He was slowed and couldn't flee in his usual manner.

He had to return home fast, to recuperate. He wiped the blood from his chin and continued.

They'd ambushed him—he'd been set up—and now he was in trouble.

He only hoped they didn't see where he went.

Finally, his front door!

He bolted inside and fell into a restorative slumber…

The lid was thrown open; the sudden light hurt. But what killed him was the wooden spike the vampire hunters drove into his heart.

S. Gepp is an Australian, with two children, two university degrees (and counting), two tertiary education diplomas, and a resumé that looks like a list of every job you could ever have without really trying, including stints as a school teacher, scientist, editor and journalist. He has also been a performance acrobat, a professional wrestler, a stand-up comedian and an actor. He has been writing for 30 years (with some publications: one novella, about 10 poems, 40-odd short stories, and a few more pending) and hopes to be a real writer if he grows up. A dull life.

Pukwudgies
by Brandy Bonifas

"The natives called them Pukwudgies," Grandmother said. "They control the dead in the burial mounds. Those woods are full of them. It's not safe."

I nodded, appeasing her superstitions, but Jake and I had our secret trysts in those woods. I couldn't stay away.

Waiting for him, I heard rustling and scraping claws. Fearful, I ran, stumbling, falling down a hill. Gathering myself, I fled. They pursued me harder, surrounding, driving me back through the woods to where I'd fallen. There, I found Jake kneeling over my lifeless body.

The Pukwudgies crept from the shadows to claim their newest dead.

Brandy Bonifas lives in Ohio with her husband and son. Her work has appeared or is forthcoming in anthologies by Clarendon House Publications, Pixie Forest Publishing, Zombie Pirate Publishing, and Blood Song Books, as well as the online publications CafeLit and Spillwords Press.
Website: www.brandybonifas.com
Facebook: brandybonifasauthor

Late Night Snack
by A.S. Charly

The curtains billow as a sudden breeze enters the room, nothing more than shadows moving in the darkness. The warmth of summer is gone now, and the cold air licking over my skin gives me goosebumps. I slip further under the blanket, trying to hide myself away, but an icy hand grips my soul.

Something screeches over the floor.

My heart races.

It lowers itself on my chest, smothering me. Breathless, I jolt…but get caught in huge silver eyes. The world spins, then there are screams everywhere, and I look at my own lifeless body from within the darkness.

A.S. Charly loves to lose herself in fantastical worlds far away between the stars, filled with magic and wonder. She also writes and draws when she is not roaming through the park with her children. Her stories have been published in various anthologies and online publications.
Facebook: A.S.Charlydreams

The Slime Monster
by Cecelia Hopkins-Drewer

The slime monster was sucking her in, assimilating her cells one by one. Now she knew what the sheep felt like when they got bogged. The pain was excruciating, and she wished she had never walked down to the dam that afternoon.

A voice called her name and her brother appeared. "Hang on, I'll get the tractor and pull you out," he said.

"No point," she replied. "Get the gun."

Slowly, inexorably, the ooze had claimed more of her body, until she knew she would never survive. The monster gurgled, its icky, green consciousness highly satisfied. The mud bubbled happily.

Cecelia Hopkins-Drewer is a speculative fiction writer, poet and scholar, who lives in Adelaide, South Australia. She has also written a Masters paper on H.P. Lovecraft, and a teenage vampire series that commences with "Mystic Evermore". Her science fiction poetry has been published in "The Mentor" a fanzine edited by Ron Clarke.
Amazon: amazon.com/Cecelia-Hopkins-Drewer/e/B071G968NM

I'll Never Fish Again
by Stephen Herczeg

"I don't know what it was. One minute he was there, the next it was dragging him under the water."

Smithy picked up his drink. His hand shook so much he could barely sip from the glass. Someone asked him to tell it again.

"We was fishing. John got a bite. Big bite. He reeled it in, got ready with the net. Then this green, scaly hand comes out the water and pulls him in. John thrashed around, before the claws dragged him under. Then the waters turned red."

Smithy gulped his scotch.

"I'll never fish again, that's for sure."

Stephen Herczeg is an IT Geek based in Canberra Australia. He has been writing for over twenty years and has completed a couple of dodgy novels, sixteen feature length screenplays and numerous short stories and scripts. His horror work has featured in Sproutlings, Hells Bells, Below the Stairs, Trickster's Treats #1 and #2, Shades of Santa, Behind the Mask, Beyond the Infinite; The Body Horror Book, Anemone Enemy, Petrified Punks and Beginnings. He has also had numerous Sherlock Holmes stories published through the Belanger Books - Sherlock Holmes anthologies.

Bogeyman
by Patrick Winters

I've been forgotten.

Once, I was great and terrible. The eye to all of little Sarah's storming fears. I would scratch my finger against the floorboards, or chuckle in my dark way, and she would cower under the covers. And if ever I reared up to reveal my horrible self, she would scream.

But Sarah no longer screams. She has grown accustomed to staying quiet, and I've since withered, left to the dusty dark beneath her mattress.

Because she no longer fears what's under her bed; she fears the bedroom door. She fears when it will open.

She fears him.

Patrick Winters is a graduate of Illinois College in Jacksonville, IL, where he earned a Bachelor of Arts degree in English Literature and Creative Writing and achieved membership into Sigma Tau Delta, an international English honors society. Winters is now a proud member of the Horror Writers Association, and his work has been published in the likes of Sanitarium Magazine, Deadman's Tome, Trysts of Fate, and other such titles. A full list of his previous publications may be found at his author's site. Website: wintersauthor.azurewebsites.net/Publications/List

Kitty
by Jensen Reed

"Get your ass out here," Leona's uncle slurred.

A deep, menacing growl rumbled through the hulking beast curled protectively around the three-year-old. Leona opened her eyes and put a small hand on his stinky, leathery hide.

"Kitty?" she asked. Memories of pain flashed through her mind as her new friend rose and slowly stepped between them, his claws clicking against the floor. Pee trickled down her uncle's pant leg as he stared open-mouthed at the grotesque beast.

"You…deserve…a…slow…death," Kitty ground out, his voice like gravel. Leona watched for a moment before snuggling under her blanket. Kitty would keep her safe.

Jensen Reed is a multi-published short story author, lead admin for Writing Bad, and mama to two boys. She dabbles in reading and writing genres but particularly enjoys feeding characters to zombies and making readers cry. Find her book links, flash fiction, and connect with her on her website. Website: authorjensenreed.wordpress.com

Old Scratch
by Terry Miller

Aubrey settled down in bed for the night. A storm raged outside, but she was safe in the comfort of her room, the nightlight shining a pale orange along the wall.

Lightning briefly turned the night into day, casting an elongated shadow on the floor. Something scratched at the window glass and knocked in discordant taps, then the sound of nails traced the footboard. The floor creaked though there was nothing there, nothing seen. Lightning flashed, the creature's face glowed, its mouth agape and eyes dark as night.

Aubrey jerked awake to a bright morning, scratches marking her cherry footboard.

Terry Miller is an author and 2017 Rhysling Award-nominated poet residing in Portsmouth, OH, USA. He has self-published a dark poetry collection on Amazon and one short story to date. His work has also appeared in Sanitarium, Devolution Z, Jitter Press, Poetry Quarterly, O Unholy Night in Deathlehem, and the 2017 Rhysling Anthology from the Science Fiction and Fantasy Poetry Association.
Facebook: tmiller2015

The Sound of Wings
by Stuart Conover

Wings flapped as Jace fled into darkness.

The monsters had torn through his friends.

Fangs, talons, ripped them apart.

Now they hunted him.

Running, he couldn't stop.

The tree line was close.

If he could make it…

The flapping came closer.

They were gaining on him.

Yet, he was almost there.

The wings beat closer as he dived into the forest.

The trees might keep them back.

Standing he broke into another run.

The sound of wings faded.

Finally, Jace stopped in the shadows and fell to his knees.

The ground wasn't dirt, but bone.

From above the flapping returned.

Stuart Conover is a father, husband, rescue dog owner, published author, blogger, journalist, horror enthusiast, comic book geek, science fiction junkie, and IT professional. With all of that to cram in daily, we have no idea if or when he sleeps or how he gets writing done! (We suspect it has to do with having evil clones.) Stuart is a Chicago native and runs the author resource Horror Tree.

The Hominian Monster
by Nerisha Kemraj

Through tiny slits Julie forced her eyes to look, hoping he wouldn't notice her awake. He towered over her—hairy arms straightening out the dress he fixed her in. She tried not to squirm or scream under his repulsive touch, but failed. He grabbed her towards a metal cage.

"I have company for you, my love. You'll be able to rest for a while," he said, flinging Julie inside as chains clinked within. She cowered.

"Help me," a familiar voice whispered.

It couldn't be.

Julie's sister who mysteriously disappeared a year ago, collapsed forward—unkempt, wan, and pregnant.

*Multi-genre (short-fiction) author, and poet, **Nerisha Kemraj**, resides in South Africa with her husband and two, mischievous daughters. She has work traditionally published/accepted in 30 publications, thus far, both print and online. She holds a BA in Communication Science from UNISA and is currently busy with a Post-Graduate Certificate in Education.*
Facebook: Nerishakemrajwriter

Divinity
by Jem McCusker

A suggestion could be fickle with its willingness to destroy weak minds. It's cloven hooves of malice and deceit seduced and prayed on those who lived for peace, for hope.

When words whispered silkily in your ear, urge you to follow your darkest thoughts in the bleak hours of the early morning it knew it had won.

The rushing water fills the tub as your mind becomes void of time and thought. The water caresses your body in gentle, blood-soaked waves. Chilled yet warm. Your chest shudders in, out, until Shinigami bows above you, gold robes flying, collecting your life.

Jem McCusker is a middle grade fiction author, living near Brisbane with her two sons and husband. Her first book Stone Guardians the Rise of Eden was released in 2018 and she is working on the sequel. She is releasing a Novella for the Four Quills writing group, A Storm of Wind and Rain series in July, 2019. She longs to be a full-time author, won't wear yellow and loves rabbits. Follow Jem on Twitter, Facebook and Instagram. Details on her website.
Website: www.jemmccusker.com

The Gardener
by Aditya Deshmukh

"Earth is like a garden. A garden so big that it houses a zillion species. But nothing is big enough for humans." I sigh. "They mess up this delicate equation of nature. Knowingly."

I snatch a blade from my surgical tray. I approach the duct-taped PM pissing in the corner.

"Like all gardens, Earth requires maintenance. Weeds need to be removed. Threats need to be eliminated. And humans—because of their uncontrollable urge of conquering and dominating—is indeed a threat."

PM crawls away from me, begging. "Ummmm...ummmm."

"They call me a monster." I cut the weed. "But I'm just a gardener."

Aditya Deshmukh is a mechanical engineering student who likes exploring the mechanics of writing as much as he likes tinkering with machines. He writes dark fiction and poetry. He is published in over three dozen anthologies and has a poetry book "Opium Hearts" and a collection of drabbles coming out soon. He likes chatting with people who share similar interests, so feel free to check him out.
Facebook: adityadeshmukhwrites
Website: www.adityadeshmukh.com

An Eye Out for the Toad People
by Shawn M. Klimek

Peering through the gem, Magdalene turned slowly, her jaw hanging, amazed.

"What can you see?" begged little Steven.

"Another world superimposed upon our own," she marvelled. "Giant toads dressed like people."

"Well, I never!" huffed a toad wearing buckled shoes. "It is you who are dressed like toads!"

An eyeless hag with a pit in the middle of her forehead sprang from the shadows, bony claws outstretched. "You've stolen my eye!" she accused. "I'm starving!"

Stepping nimbly to one side, little Steven pushed his scout knife into her heart.

"No more eating toads for you," said the Fairy Prince, unmasking.

Shawn M. Klimek is the middle child of seven creative siblings, a globetrotting, U.S. military spouse, an internationally best-selling short-story writer, a poet, and butler to a Maltese. Almost one hundred of his stories or poems have been published in digital magazines or anthologies, including BHP's Deep Space and the first six books in the Dark Drabbles series.
Website: jotinthedark.blogspot.com
Facebook: shawnmklimekauthor

When Dinner Knocks
by Holly Saiki

Staring in horror as Dell transformed into a werewolf, the salesman stood frozen in place. His mind yelled at him to run, but he couldn't. A scream dying to a rattle when he opened his mouth.

"Thank you so much, I don't have to worry about dinner tonight," Dell said, drool slavering down his fangs. Sunlight making his claws and yellow eyes shine with a luminous, eerie glow.

With a snap of his fearsome jaws, he ripped the salesman's throat from his neck. The victim's body slumped on Dell's welcome mat with a dull thud, blood seeping onto the porch.

Holly Saiki is a part-time retail worker living in Kapolei, HI on the Island of Oahu. Her fiction has appeared in Café Irreal, The Stray Branch, Ink Stains Magazine, Brilliant Flash Fiction, TANSTAAFL Press' "Enter the Rebirth" and is forthcoming in Words and Brushes Volume one. She's currently at work writing a super hero novel called Serendipity City Adventures: Shotgun Annie and Blood Gun vs the Meditators.
Twitter: @Rayshell33
Facebook: writingden

The New Mattress
By Olivia Arieti

Going to bed had become an obsession for Rupert; he wondered if it was due to the new water mattress or to his heavy conscience. Nothing he could do about the latter for murder was his job, he was paid for that. Whenever the boss called, the killer responded.

Every night the sensation of needles pricking his body woke him up. Enough! He would get rid of the mattress the following morning.

The resolution let him finally rest until a myriad of monstrous green creatures crawled out, snaked all over and with their shining teeth started devouring the criminal's flesh.

Olivia Arieti has a degree from the University of Pisa and lives in Torre del Lago Puccini, Italy, with her family. Besides being a published playwright, she loves writing retellings of fairy tales, and at the same time is intrigued by supernatural and horror themes. Her stories appeared in several magazines and anthologies like Enchanted Conversations, Enchanted Tales Literary Magazine, Fantasia Divinity Magazine, Cliterature, Medieval Nightmares, Static Movement, 100 Doors To Madness Forgotten Tomb Press, Black Cats Horrified Press, Bloody Ghost Stories Full Moon Books, Death And Decorations Thirteen O'Clock Press, Infective Ink, Pandemonium Press, Pussy Magic Magazine.*

The Siren
by K.T. Tate

I should've killed it. Curse the meteor that birthed that bioluminescent mushroom, jellyfish monstrosity into my pond. It was so fascinating at first.

It grew quickly, decimating the pond life. Tadpoles, frogs and fish, all caught by its opalescent tendrils.

Weeks later, corpses appeared on the bank. Hollowed out, sucker marked things that had once been rabbits, cats and foxes.

Then it started to sing.

Beguiling music now pours from its oscillating frills. I tie myself to the chair like Odysseus. The sound of the gate incites panic. I can only watch, sobbing, as the child totters towards the pond.

K.T. Tate lives in Cambridgeshire in the UK. She writes mainly weird fiction, cosmic horror and strange monster stories.
Website: eldritchhollow.wordpress.com
Tumblr: eldritch-hollow.tumblr.com

Night-mare
by Daniel Braithwaite

Another night, the room was humid, and the moonlight provided the only illumination. Chest inflamed, as I tossed and turned.

Within the shadows, I spotted movement.

A figure hobbled out, a woman, skin pallor mortis and taut, eyes glazed grey. The comforter became denser than a gravestone. I thrashed, but my limbs wouldn't budge, I'm imprisoned in her death gaze.

In my peripheral vision, I noticed another of these creatures; as it crawled up my bed before it perched atop my chest. The cloud of its eyes revealed the nature of its visit, while I witnessed my essence drift away.

Daniel Braithwaite is a speculative fiction writer, with a primary focus on horror. He hails from Toronto but currently resides further North in the city of Barrie. You can read his work in bathroom stalls or the 4,000-word story carved into an old oak tree next to a babbling brook; it is difficult to find though. Also, you can read more of his work in the Sirens Call Publications: Issue 28, Issue 32, and Issue 36.
Facebook: dan.r.braithwaite

Ear Worm
by John Saxton

I half wake. Cold. Damp. Supine.

Smoke and death impregnate the air.

A strange, unearthly droning invades my mind, inducing me to shake my head violently.

Aware of a sickening stench, eyes focussing slowly, I see the lifeless enemy lying next to me; the man's horror-struck face is inches from my own.

Something bloated, viscous, pulsing, slithers out of the corpse's blood-blackened ear. And into mine.

Searing, white-hot agony—the relentless, high-pitched buzzing intensifies, amplifies!

Staggering to my feet, I lurch on unsteady legs across No-Man's-Land. Hoping the bullets cut me down before the burrowing ear worm reaches my brain.

John Saxton hails from Yorkshire, UK, where he is happily married, with two sons. He has had over 50 short horror stories published in the independent press, including his own collection: 'Bloodshot'. He writes mainly after dark... Twitter: @jsaxtonwriter

Petrified Wood
by J. Farrington

Have you ever taken a stroll through a forest on a lazy afternoon? Admired nature in all its beauty? Ever felt *not* alone?

It's alive, you know…the forest around you. The trees speak to one another when you're not around, about how close you were to danger without realising.

About how you were within an inch of your life, the Archaic Beast close enough to pounce. The trees too petrified to help.

So, when you hear a twig snap, or the leaves suddenly rustle…

Be sure to thank the forest on your way out. You were so close to death...

***J. Farrington** is an aspiring author from the West Midlands, UK. His genre of choice is horror; whether that be psychological, suspense, supernatural or straight up weird, he'll give it a shot! He has loved writing from a young age but has only publicly been spreading his darker thoughts and sinister imagination via social platforms since 2018. If you would like to view his previous work, or merely lurk in the shadows...watching, you can keep up to date with future projects by spirit board or alternatively, the following;*
Twitter: @SurvivorTrench
Reddit: TrenchChronicles

Prey
by A.R. Johnston

He stalked his prey with cunning and precise motions. There would be no way this one was getting away from him. Not that she even knew that she was being stalked and tracked. He chuckled at the thought. The surprise of the moment was almost the highlight of it all and, oh my, would she be surprised.

She would have no idea that her death would be his crowning glory. Her blood would be his badge of honour. Her death would prove to all the others that he belonged.

He sprang. She screamed, and it was music to his ears.

A.R. Johnston is a small-town girl from Nova Scotia, Canada. Her style of writing is considered Urban Fantasy. Her first major publication is part of an anthology called First Love and she has several more titles lined up. She is a lover of coffee, good tv shows, horror flicks, and reader of books. She pretends to be a writer when real life doesn't get in the way. Pesky full-time job and adulting!

The Children of Camazotz
by Patrick Winters

Matías wound through the darkness, walking deeper into the Belizean forest; when he heard the murmuring of voices up ahead, he knew he was in the right place.

Soon the trees gave way, and he stepped into a clearing, where a dozen others stood, naked and patiently waiting. He took his place among them—these total strangers, these brothers and sisters of his—and stripped bare.

Minutes passed. Others arrived.

Then, when a great, screeching shadow eclipsed the moon overhead, they took the form of their Father, and they followed him up into the skies—to feast as a family.

Patrick Winters is a graduate of Illinois College in Jacksonville, IL, where he earned a Bachelor of Arts degree in English Literature and Creative Writing and achieved membership into Sigma Tau Delta, an international English honors society. Winters is now a proud member of the Horror Writers Association, and his work has been published in the likes of Sanitarium Magazine, Deadman's Tome, Trysts of Fate, and other such titles. A full list of his previous publications may be found at his author's site. Website: wintersauthor.azurewebsites.net/Publications/List

Settling
by K.R. Monin

Now you lay down to sleep, waiting to hear the familiar creak of footless stairs and windless sighs. You are waiting for poetry, for the comforting rhythm of doors that glide inward and snap shut with sharp drafts.

You don't dwell on the comfort of regular disruptions. Your mind is distant, following the night train's song and speeding off to warmer places where there are better-paying jobs.

What would you do for a salary? Spill a few harmless untruths? Offer something you wouldn't share with your spouse? Conjure an ancient shadow that blends with the sights and sounds of night?

K.R. Monin writes near-future sci-fi and speculative fiction. She lives in Pittsburgh, identifies as a beer snob, and thrives on wanderlust.
Twitter: @kunderscoremons

Wing Bone
by Simon Clarke

A sound in the dark. There are noises, always, of the house bedding down.

I'm alone at night, it's not safe otherwise, being hunted and haunted for years.

The bedroom door slowly opens. Through a foetid haze stands a winged, clawed, skeletal figure. A voice crawling from earth's unholiest place summons me to follow, youthful rituals claiming a last soul.

Memories return—the old ritual. I grab the carved wing bone flute and blow eerie sounds

The piping changes. The sounds are piercing. I scream soundlessly.

Later, dawn whispers me awake. I lay still, waiting for life to begin.

Simon Clarke was born in and raised and currently resides in East Anglia, United Kingdom. He has been writing fiction for at least five years and regularly submits to UK and international publications as well as reading short pieces and poetry at open mic events. He is currently working on his first novel and continues to write short stories and poetry.

They Never Look Up
by Neen Cohen

A dark silhouette against the night perches on the corner of the building. Below the crowd dwindles to those who don't believe in creatures of the night, those who don't believe in her.

She spots her prey, flicks her wings out. The sound of slapping leather catches the man's attention. He stops and looks around. He doesn't look up.

He walks faster. Not enough.

Fast and swift she leaves the building. The man looks up.

He thinks about screaming before wings cocoon him like a lover's embrace. Fangs pierce his neck. The vampire sighs at the taste of his blood.

Neen Cohen lives in Brisbane with her partner, son and fur babies. She is a writer of LGBTQI, dark fantasy and horror short stories and has a Bachelor of Creative Industries from QUT. She can often be found writing while sitting against a tombstone or tree in any number of graveyards.
Facebook: Neen-Cohen-Author-424700821629629
Website: wordbubblessite.wordpress.com

One Way to Keep a Promise
by Austin P. Sheehan

Dropping my wine glass, blood streaming out my nose, I collapsed to the floor. He loomed above me, eyes black with malice, a sick grin on his face. I flinched as he grabbed me, dragging me up onto the bed, too weak to fight back.

"Okay," I whimpered through my raw, aching throat. "I'm yours. I promise I'll never even look at another man again."

"I know, baby." He smiled. His cool, calculating voice sent chills up my spine. My heart sank as he raised the stem of the broken wine glass above my face. "This time, I believe you."

Austin P. Sheehan is a writer of speculative fiction, a lover of language, literature and '90s TV. Armed with a psychology degree, he went into the world to study humanity, and now prefers the company of his wife and their greyhounds. He grew up in the valleys of Victoria's high country, and despite living in Melbourne, always feels at home amongst the mountains. You'll often find mountains in his stories, whether they're sci-fi, fantasy or alternative history.
Website: austinpsheehan.com
Twitter: @AustinPSheehan

The Hill Beast
by Alexander Pyles

I wanted to believe in the beast in the hills for Greg's sake, but I just couldn't. Yet, I found myself on the side of a mountain looking with him. He had gone to grab firewood, but the sun was quickly setting now. No cell service out here either, of course.

The idiot probably walked off a cliff or was picking flowers. The man could be such a hopeless romantic. I'll be damned if I was going to be left behind.

I was about to leave our camp when snarls filled the air. Greg's bloodied hat landed at my feet.

Alexander Pyles resides in IL with his wife and children. He holds an MA in Philosophy and an MFA in Writing Popular Fiction. His short story chapbook titled, "Milo (01001101 01101001 01101100 01101111)," from Radix Media, is due out fall 2019. His other short fiction has appeared on 101fiction.org, River and South Review, and other venues. Website: www.pylesofbooks.com Twitter: @Pylesofbooks

The Watermelon Contest
by J.M. Meyer

"The *winner*…, Jay Bristow with his 360-pound watermelon. Don't kill anyone rolling that baby home."

Laughter.

"I brought my axe. I plan on sharing it here."

Applause.

With the hotdog eating, best pie and fattest sow contest complete, Jay wielded his axe above the pregnant fruit.

"What *did* you use for fertiliser, Chernobyl Soil?"

Uncomfortable laughter.

"Nope, but I did use a 'grow giant fruit *or* die spell' I found online."

Cheers.

Watermelon shrapnel, bloody pulp and millions of carnivorous legged seeds engulfed anything with a pulse after metal hit fruit.

Screams.

Jay always mixed up "*or*" with "*and*."

J.M. Meyer is writer, artist and small business owner living in New York., where she received her master's degree from Teacher's College, Columbia University. Jacqueline loves the science fiction and horror genres. Reading Ray Bradbury was a mind-blowing experience for her in 8th grade. Alfred Hitchcock and Rod Serling were the horror heroes of her youth. Mercedes M. Yardley is her current horror writing hero. Jacqueline also enjoys the company of her husband Bruce and their three children, Julia, Emma and Lauren. Jacqueline's mantra: The only time it's too late to try something new is when you are dead.
Website: jmoranmeyer.net
Twitter: @moran_meyer

Rotting Zombie
by Thomas Sturgeon Jr.

It's already been several days since I was last bitten and turned into a zombie. I walk around as my flesh is rotting away, the stench of death as I stumble around looking for flesh that I so crave.

My sunken eyes that still hint at what was once the beautiful life of an artist.

Now I bite into the flesh of my victim, with blood dripping from my jaws. There's more of us each day.

When we come out in hordes, death is knocking on your doors. We come in all shapes and sizes.

We are coming your way.

Thomas Sturgeon Jr. began writing at 13 years old. He loves to read and spend time with his family and friends. He loves horror movies and fiction. He currently lives in Chatsworth, Georgia and wants more out of life. He's been published before in Weird Mask magazine and by Deadman's Tome. His short stories that were published were "The Dead City" and "Disturbed Valentine". He currently is at work on a Horror short story collection and he is loved by his family and friends. Despite being told by his teachers that he would never be published, he has proved them wrong.

Donor
by Paul Warmerdam

Eyes finally open, Jane couldn't breathe. The room was cold and silent. There were others lying still under their veils, a John and another Jane. She tried to remember, but there was only nothingness.

She felt her skin and winced when she found the scars. There was a report nearby. She read as voices sounded in the hallway beyond. They argued about something they didn't understand.

Jane understood. *They took it all.* She tried to scream in rage but knew she would never find her voice again. The doctors were close when Jane couldn't bear the emptiness inside any longer.

Paul Warmerdam is a Dutch-American with decades of experience writing stories, who only recently decided to start submitting them. He lives in the Netherlands, where there's plenty of rainy hours shut indoors with a story in mind.

Killer Garden
by C.L. Williams

I go to my garden to water my plants. I check everything to make sure all is copasetic.

My only problem is my squash bit me while I was checking it. The squash ripened before everything else and is ready to wreak havoc. I tell it that it must wait.

Everything is good and I can now share my vegetables with all. Little do the people know, these vegetables will be the ones eating them! They were grown with one thought in mind, ending the human race. I even left it in the card as well; en*joy my killer garden!*

C.L. Williams is an independent author from central Virginia. He has written eight poetry books, four novellas, one novel, and a contributor to multiple anthologies, with the most recent appearance being an all-ages anthology titled Temoli from Thazbook. His most recent poetry book, The Paradox Complex, features the poem "Sad Crying Clown" that is now a video on YouTube directed by Matthew Mark Hunter of MMH Productions. C.L. Williams is currently working on his first sci-fi book, an all-ages book titled Novo: Away from Earth. When not writing, C.L. Williams is reading and sharing the work of other independent authors. Facebook: writer434
Twitter: @writer_434

The Trumpet Calls
by Martin Eastland

The librarian walked 'the stacks', pushing her little cart as she went. Turning the corner into the Humanities section, she saw him standing there.

He looked good from the back. Well-proportioned, with a nice, tight ass.

Then he turned around.

She drew a sharp intake of air. His eyes burned red, lapsed in a storm of fury, ocular bonfires raging against his corneas.

Tilting his head, his jaw dropped open, two sharp canines protruding beneath his gums, saliva dripping from his tongue. Drawing her closer.

He was gliding towards her, the trumpets in her mind heralding her almost certain demise.

*Born in Glasgow, Scotland, **Martin Eastland** began his writing career at the age of 12, his only outlet allowing him to escape a less than harmonious childhood. Almost 30 years later, he has gone from strength to strength as a writer, expanding into new areas, but remaining loyal to his preferred genres of horror, and the suspense-thriller. He enjoys mainly short stories and flash fiction as he views it as being beneficial for his future development as an author. He is happily married with four children, and lives with his wife in Shropshire, England.*
Facebook: Martin-Eastland-245154596385827

The Beast
by Michael D. Lackey

The Beast caused chaos again last night.

Broken windows, trash strewn everywhere and the smell of despair still lingering on the morning air.

The police said they have seen him, tried to do their duty. But the Beast is smart, he eludes capture.

I know I can stop him. I am the only one capable of putting an end to all the horror and heartbreak; the bloodshed and tears. I know where to find the Beast, so I go to confront him.

"This has to stop. You need help... I need help," I say as I gaze into the mirror.

Michael D. Lackey is a fantasy and Sci-fi writer. He is the author of The Bad Seed: Battle for the Heavens and The Key of Knowledge. He enjoys creating worlds for new readers and old to escape to and just have fun.
Website: www.michaellackeyauthor.com

Late Night Drinks
by David Bowmore

"Pint please," the vampire said.

The claws of the werewolf made drawing the blood easy, if a little messy.

"Quiet tonight," said the vampire, after paying.

"I know. It's their fault, they unnerve the regulars."

The vampire looked sideways at a group of zombies in the corner of the room.

"Weird, are they not?" said the vampire.

"It's unnatural, is what it is," said the werewolf. "They don't drink or eat. They just sit there groaning." He lifted the still living victim's arm and helped himself to a couple of fingers.

"But they're no trouble?"

"Nah. Not in my pub."

David Bowmore has lived here, there and everywhere, but now lives in Yorkshire with his wonderful wife and a small white poodle. He has worn many hats in his time; head chef, teacher and landscape gardener. His first collection of short stories 'The Magic of Deben Market' is available from Clarendon House.
Website: davidbowmore.co.uk
Facebook: davidbowmoreauthor

Creation
by Elizabeth Montague

He looked upon his work, years of research and experimentation culminating in this point. His heart thumped, sweat beading on his forehead, savouring the moment of anticipation.

A spark was all it needed to bring life to such a complex machine. He wondered what it would achieve. He could peer into the future but he resisted, igniting the spark and watching it rise into a living thing.

It was beautiful. He couldn't resist looking into its future as he released it into his world.

He was shaking when he saw the horrors that lay ahead.

He lamented, "I've created Man."

Elizabeth Montague is a multi-genre author from Hertfordshire, England. Her short story collection, Dust and Glitter, was released by Clarendon House Publications in May 2019. She has previously featured in nine anthologies from the same publisher alongside publications from Scout Media, Black Hare Press and Iron Faerie Publishing. She is currently working on her first novel alongside continuing to produce short stories in several genres.
Website: elizabethmontagueauthor.wordpress.com
Facebook: elizabethmontaguewrites

Bad Date
by Dawn DeBraal

Gretchen slammed her front door twisting the deadbolt. "Computer Match" dating site, totally bogus. The guy ordered his steak extremely rare, wolfing it down. Gretchen was not amused. After dinner as he escorted her to her car, he howled at the moon. Yes, howled. He asked Gretchen if she would like to go somewhere else? Gretchen politely declined. Going in for a kiss goodnight, he put his paws on her.

Relieved to be home, Gretchen felt much better until she pulled back the curtain showing a full moon, after hearing a howl that sounded strikingly familiar to her bad date.

Dawn DeBraal lives in rural Wisconsin with her husband, two rat terriers, and a cat. She successfully raised two children (meaning they didn't return to the nest!) After many years serving the government at the Federal and County level, she recently retired. Having extra time on her hands she started to write after a paralyzed vocal cord took her ability to speak for two months. Not finding her voice, she discovered that her love of telling a good story could be written. Her works have been published in Palm-sized press, Spillwords, Mercurial Stories, Potato Soup Journal, and Blood Song Books.

Car Trouble
by Austin P. Sheehan

"Car trouble?" he asked, stepping from his ute. His weather-beaten face and grease-stained hands told me he knew more about cars than me. Not much of a stretch, though. Most people do. "Well, what's wrong with it, mate? Speak up!"

"Uh, could be the alternator," I shrugged.

"Then you're proper farked." He grinned. "Go on, give us a look." As he nudged me out of the way, I grabbed the hood support, collapsing the bonnet on him. Pushing down hard, I pressed him against the engine.

After the screaming stopped, I drove off in his ute. I wasn't done yet.

Austin P. Sheehan is a writer of speculative fiction, a lover of language, literature and '90s TV. Armed with a psychology degree, he went into the world to study humanity, and now prefers the company of his wife and their greyhounds. He grew up in the valleys of Victoria's high country, and despite living in Melbourne, always feels at home amongst the mountains. You'll often find mountains in his stories, whether they're sci-fi, fantasy or alternative history.
Website: austinpsheehan.com
Twitter: @AustinPSheehan

During the Game
by Gabriella Balcom

Watching a football game on television, Robert crammed popcorn into his mouth. He chugged beer, crushed his empty can with one hand, discarded it, and popped open a new one.

"Bad call!" he yelled. "Stupid referee, are you blind?"

Totally engrossed in the game, Robert didn't notice smoke seeping into his home through an open window. It coalesced into a swaying, cat-like shape. Yellow eyes appeared, glittering with malice.

The entity ducked down behind a recliner when Robert stood during a commercial. The man hurried to get more beer from his refrigerator and didn't notice the creature moving toward him.

Gabriella Balcom lives in Texas with her family, loves reading and writing, and thinks she was born with a book in her hands. She works in a mental health field, and writes fantasy, horror/thriller, romance, children's stories, and sci-fi. She likes travelling, music, good shows, photography, history, interesting tales, and animals. Gabriella says she's a sucker for a great story and loves forests, mountains, and back roads which might lead who knows where. She has a weakness for lasagne, garlic bread, tacos, cheese, and chocolate, but not necessarily in that order.
Facebook: GabriellaBalcom.lonestarauthor

Exotic
by Donald Jacob Uitvlugt

"I must have her."

The proprietor of Big Jim's Aquatics tapped the tank. "Ugly sonofa. But nobody's seen anything like it."

"Not under these stars."

"My supplier netted it in the Pacific. Ate up half the stock in his hold. It's not cheap."

"I'd sell my soul for her."

Big Jim grinned, tasting the impending sale. "Take a month until the quarantine's—"

A shot thundered, passed through Big Jim, shattered the aquarium beyond. With a rush of foetid water, the creature tumbled onto the body.

"I must have her now..."

From the floor, the creature laughed as it fed.

First appeared in *Necrotic Tissue*, issue 9, 2010

*Donald Jacob Uitvlugt lives on neither coast of the United States, but mostly in a haunted memory palace of his own design. His short fiction has appeared in numerous print and online venues, including Cirsova Magazine and the Flame Tree Press anthology Murder Mayhem. He works primarily in speculative fiction, though he loves blending and stretching genres. He strives to write what he calls "haiku fiction," stories that are small in scale but big in impact.
Website: haikufiction.blogspot.com
Twitter: @haikufictiondju*

To Sleep, Perchance to Dream
by Shelly Jarvis

I come through the strange place between asleep and awake. Those precious seconds before your mind lets go into unconsciousness. I know you've felt me wriggling through the crack. You've even jolted awake with the sensation of falling. You were falling. But don't worry: I'll catch you, with claws.

Once I slip through that sliver of opportunity, you're mine. Your dreams become my playground, your nightmares honey on my tongue. Sometimes I thrash about in your head, just to watch you squirm. To wake you, the torment of the minutes sneaking by while you should be sleeping.

Tonight, I come.

Shelly Jarvis is a speculative fiction author from West Virginia, US. She found a life-long love of sci-fi and fantasy in the 3rd grade when she found Madeleine L'Engle's "A Wrinkle in Time." Shelly is an avid reader, a Whovian, the ideal viewer of dog rescue videos, and undoubtedly Ravenclaw. She currently has two YA sci-fi books available for purchase on Amazon.
Website: www.ShellyJarvis.com

The Grinning Shadow
by J.D. Bell

What is it that lies hidden in the dark, deep within the shadows? How can you be afraid of something you cannot see? But there is something there. You feel it. Sense it. The shadows move and swirl around you. Your mind plays tricks on you. The dark is teasing you.

Then you see it. A shapeless form with gleaming white teeth. Razor-sharp fangs float in the dark. The evil grin moves toward you, laughing at you. The laughter changes to a hideous sound. It is the sound of bones being crushed by the evil grin in the dark.

J.D. Bell is an award-winning, internationally published, author of flash fiction and short stories. He recently retired from the world of writing advertising copy and is now enjoying the universe of creative fiction.
Facebook: jim.writes.stories
Twitter: @JimBell58

The Big Snack
by R.G. Halstead

The kid was scared shitless. But he was smart. He would find a way to get safely from his bedroom to the bathroom, but he had to hurry.

It came to him.

"Mama."

No response.

"Mama!"

Still no response.

The boy screeched like he was in horrific pain. As if some sort of monster had him as its lunch. The woman came running into his bedroom. "What is it now, you little bastard?" his drunk mother growled.

The monsters under his bed—that his parents had always warned him about—grabbed their late-night snack. Much bigger than the boy.

R.G. Halstead, a 63-year-old, takes to writing late in his life. Influences? Those old Alfred Hitchcock Mystery Magazines from the late 1950s and the 1960s with the great twisty endings. Love them.

Redcap
by Vonnie Winslow Crist

"It's not personal," explained the thickset, mannish creature, "but my cap has faded."

Lonnie struggled to loosen the grip of the Border goblin's clawed hand. But Redcap's hold was unbreakable.

"Please," he managed to say.

"I am pleased," responded Redcap as he clanked down the staircase into the abandoned castle's cellar in iron boots. "You appear a healthy lad. Should be plenty of blood for the dyeing."

The grisly-haired goblin held Ronnie above a stone vat, lifted his pikestaff, asked, "Any last words?"

"Wait!"

"Nope," said Redcap.

Later, the goblin was happy with the deep red colour of his cap.

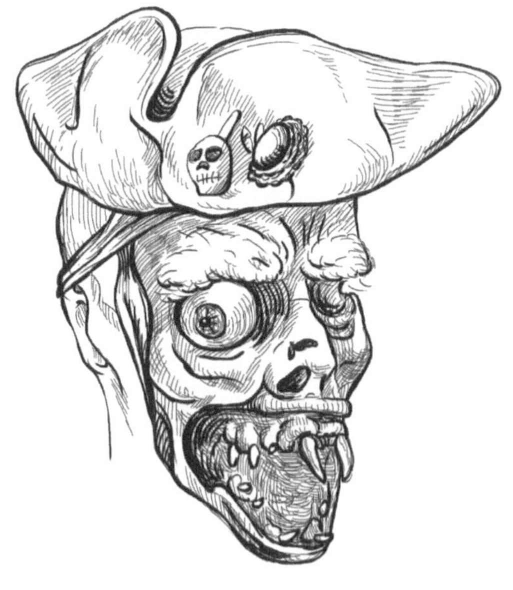

Vonnie Winslow Crist is author of The Enchanted Dagger, Owl Light, The Greener Forest, Murder on Marawa Prime, and other award-winning books. Her fiction is included in "Amazing Stories," "Cast of Wonders," "Outposts of Beyond," Killing It Softly 2, Defending the Future - Dogs of War, Midnight Masquerade, Chaos of Hard Clay, and elsewhere. A cloverhand who has found so many four-leafed clovers she keeps them in jars, Vonnie strives to celebrate the power of myth in her writing.
Website: www.vonniewinslowcrist.com

Cave Mouth
by Shelly Jarvis

"I'm stuck. My shoulders can't get through."

I turn my head, trying to shine my light into the narrow passage. I haven't been to this cave before, but Brendon says it's amazing once you get in. And he made it, despite being a bit bigger than me.

"You've gotta twist a little more. You're almost there."

I close my eyes, trying to relax. I've been stuck before, but never this bad. I breathe in. A foul, wet smell hits my face. "Oh god, what's that stench?"

"Just your friend. Humans make me gassy."

My world tips forward and I fall.

Shelly Jarvis is a speculative fiction author from West Virginia, US. She found a life-long love of sci-fi and fantasy in the 3rd grade when she found Madeleine L'Engle's "A Wrinkle in Time." Shelly is an avid reader, a Whovian, the ideal viewer of dog rescue videos, and undoubtedly Ravenclaw. She currently has two YA sci-fi books available for purchase on Amazon.
Website: www.ShellyJarvis.com

Déjà Devoré
by Joel R. Hunt

Too late, I realise the monster doesn't just feed on flesh. It feeds on memories. Perhaps I've realised that before, and it devoured that knowledge from within me. Soon I'll be nothing—an empty husk, no past, no hopes, no dreams. I have to escape. I have to keep running.

Have I seen that tree before?

Behind me, branches crunch. With a jolt, I realise it's right behind me. Chasing me. I run before I'm devoured.

But where am I? Where am I running to? Everything looks strangely familiar.

Too late, I realise the monster doesn't just feed on flesh…

Joel R. Hunt is a writer from the UK who dabbles in the darker aspects of life, particularly through horror, science fiction and the supernatural. He has been published here and there (though likely nowhere you've heard of) and hopes to have released his first anthology of short stories later this year.
Twitter: @JoelRHunt1
Reddit: JRHEvilInc

Birth of a Breath-Eater
by Jonathan Inbody

Carson doubled over, coughing violently. There was something in his lungs, something he couldn't cough up. His throat pushed outward suddenly as something crawled up from his windpipe into the back of his mouth. As he breathlessly choked and retched, he wondered what had been in those herbal cigarettes. A tar-covered homunculi pulled itself out of his open mouth, slick with blood from Carson's shredded throat. It tapped its jagged claws on the wooden floor, then scrambled off under a nearby couch as blood pooled around Carson's crumpled body. His daughter had been right after all; smoking *can* kill you.

Jonathan Inbody is a filmmaker, author, and podcaster from Buffalo, New York. He enjoys B-movies, pen and paper RPGs, and New Wave Science Fiction novels. His short story "Dying Feels Like Slowly Sinking" is due to be published in the anthology Deteriorate from Whimsically Dark Publishing. Jon can be heard every other week on his improvisational movie pitch podcast X Meets Y.
Website: xmeetsy.libsyn.com

Confrontation
by G. Allen Wilbanks

"I told you not to come here."

"I know," said Kristin. "But I had to see for myself. Is it true?"

Michael bared his teeth, revealing two pale white fangs.

"You know this means I can't let you leave here alive," Michael told her, sadly. "I wish you had listened to me."

Kristin nodded distractedly at the threat. "So, vampires are real. I guess I really shouldn't be so surprised. If werewolves are real, why not vampires?"

"Werewolves?" asked Michael, a puzzled expression crossing his features.

"Werewolves," repeated Kristin, feeling the familiar tingling that meant the change had already begun.

G. Allen Wilbanks is a member of the Horror Writers Association (HWA) and has published over 50 short stories in various magazines and on-line venues. He is the author of two short story collections, and the novel, When Darkness Comes.
Website: www.gallenwilbanks.com
Blog: DeepDarkThoughts.com

To Summon the Sea
by Alexander Pyles

The Naga came. Scales glittering like the seafoam behind them, eyes like polished pearls. They slithered through the sand, surging up to our village.

We were not ready.

Frantically, my countrymen grasped muskets and rushed into the street. They only met a violent end. I watched their blood flow through the streets. Fang and claw rent coats and flesh alike, with ease. It would not be long before the village was flotsam.

I took no pleasure in watching the massacre as the denizens of the abyss reclaimed what had been stolen. It was right to summon them, despite my regret.

Alexander Pyles resides in IL with his wife and children. He holds an MA in Philosophy and an MFA in Writing Popular Fiction. His short story chapbook titled, "Milo (01001101 01101001 01101100 01101111)," from Radix Media, is due out fall 2019. His other short fiction has appeared on 101fiction.org, River and South Review, and other venues. Website: www.pylesofbooks.com Twitter: @Pylesofbooks

The Changeling
by T.A. Sola

The familiar stench of paraffin filled my cramped, dirty cell.

The fumes burned my lungs, made my head spin and my chest heave. I thought, as I fell to my knees and clawed at my throat, that this time I would die.

But I didn't. To die would to be forgiven, and that I did not deserve.

I stared up at the window. Too high for me to reach, too high to glimpse the creature that tormented me. But I didn't need to see. I knew what it was, who it pretended to be.

"I'm sorry," I said. "I'm sorry."

T.A. Sola is a publication designer and writer of speculative fiction from Tallahassee, Florida. His previous works can be found in Three Crows Magazine Issue 2 and TL;DR Press's 2018 Horror Anthology Nope.

Revenge of the Worm Lord
by Shawn M. Klimek

Those noisy crickets! Saddened by little Mark's insomnia, the Night Worm wriggled from its muddy lair, squirmed upstairs, then peered over the top of the bed at the boy's restless silhouette. To ease his suffering, the Night Worm thrust its head and tail into the child's two ear canals: a snug fit.

Soon, the boy fell asleep and began to dream of worms: worm clusters, worm multitudes, and ultimately—the fearsome Worm Lord.

His parents were relieved to see their son finally rested. Their new worry was his tendency to bite off the heads of tweeting birds before shouting, "Revenge!"

Shawn M. Klimek is the middle child of seven creative siblings, a globetrotting, U.S. military spouse, an internationally best-selling short-story writer, a poet, and butler to a Maltese. Almost one hundred of his stories or poems have been published in digital magazines or anthologies, including BHP's Deep Space and the first six books in the Dark Drabbles series.
Website: jotinthedark.blogspot.com
Facebook: shawnmklimekauthor

After Midnight
by Matthew M. Montelione

The gremlins of my suburban neighbourhood stayed hidden until the noise was too loud for them to handle. One fateful summer night, my next-door neighbour hosted a party. He blasted music past midnight, the sounds clanged throughout my usually quiet street. Around one o'clock in the morning, the noise stopped. My neighbours were relieved, until days later, when we noticed the smell.

Upon entering the house, the cops found several dead with their mouths sewn shut. The stereo system laid in pieces in pools of blood.

The gremlins had silenced them.

From then on, nobody spoke a word after midnight.

Matthew M. Montelione is a horror writer born and raised on Long Island in New York. His stories have been published in Quoth the Raven: A Contemporary Reimagining of the Works of Edgar Allan Poe, Thuggish Itch: Devilish, MONSTERS: A Horror Microfiction Anthology, Eerie Christmas, and other titles. Matthew is also an American Revolution historian who focuses on the local experiences of Loyalists on Long Island. His work on the subject has been published in Long Island History Journal and Journal of the American Revolution. Matthew lives with his wife in New York.
Website: maybeevils.com
Twitter: @maybeevils

Welcome Home
by Sinister Sweetheart

The mother mourned for her child, never leaving her chair by the window. Her son had disappeared thirteen years ago on that very day. The police were less than helpful, no one understood. People never knew the boy, a shut in like his mother.

Things were different; on the 13th anniversary, something *did* come home. It was a hulking figure; a bipedal beast with the face of a rotted sheep. The beast's cloven hooves clicked their way across the tiles.

He lifted the woman high above the floor. Tears streamed down her face. "My dear son, how you have grown!"

*Since **Sinister Sweetheart** made her first post to a popular Internet forum, she's taken the horror community by storm. Her ability to create, terrify, and drive home her stories is insurmountable. Sinister Sweetheart's published works can be found in multiple anthologies for all to read, but be forewarned, if you do... you may want to call your therapist after, her stories are terrifying, disturbing and devilishly unsettling. She is not only a fright visually, but also has a creepy tentacle in horror podcasting as well. Sinister Sweetheart writes, voice acts and is the media director of the Scarecrow Tales podcast.*
Website: Sinistersweetheart.wixsite.com/sinistersweetheart
Facebook: NMBrownStories

No Rest for the Wicked
by John H. Dromey

Former mates had an interstellar video chat.

"I see you're in your altered state. Does that mean your extra-terrestrial enterprise is a howling success?"

"Not really. My schedule entails a heavier-than-anticipated workload. I haven't had a decent night's rest since I arrived. I'm paid a generous per diem, but I can't wait for my sideshow-attraction contract to expire."

"Is there a silver lining?"

"No, but I suppose that's a good thing—having no threat of a fatal argent allergy flare-up."

"What's your problem then?"

"I'm exhausted! This planet has so many moons being a werewolf here is a full-time job!"

John H. Dromey was born in northeast Missouri, USA. He enjoys reading—mysteries in particular—and writing in a variety of genres. He's had short fiction published in Alfred Hitchcock's Mystery Magazine, Martian Magazine, Stupefying Stories Showcase, Thriller Magazine, Unfit Magazine, and elsewhere, as well as in a number of anthologies, including Chilling Horror Short Stories (Flame Tree Publishing, 2015).

Carrion, My Wayward Son
by Beth W. Patterson

He was too proud to eat carrion, so he slaughtered the scavengers. Buzzards were slow to respond, and they seldom feared him until it was too late.

It would be harder to kill the CEO of some pharmaceutical company that fed on the sick and dying. So, he practiced on those great black birds, eating feathers, bones, and all.

Flunking out of Clown College had made him bitter, but he was determined to make a difference in the world. It was what his father wanted.

He would soon take down the fat cats, with a painted smile and death breath.

Beth W. Patterson was a full-time musician for over two decades before diving into the world of writing, a process she describes as "fleeing the circus to join the zoo". She is the author of the books Mongrels and Misfits, and The Wild Harmonic, and a contributing writer to twenty anthologies. Patterson has performed in eighteen countries, expanding her perspective as she goes. Her playing appears on over a hundred and sixty albums, soundtracks, videos, commercials, and voice-overs (including seven solo albums of her own). She lives in New Orleans, Louisiana with her husband Josh Paxton, jazz pianist extraordinaire.
Website: www.bethpattersonmusic.com
Facebook: bethodist

Thy Will be Gone
by J.W. Garrett

The wraith dug into the mush of his mind, the delicious task all but done.

Sleep was the perfect time to break their determination. To dominate… Command…

Night after night he muddled the humans' brains, wrestled their thoughts, built his army. Desires, outcomes fell under his control. A sneer twisted his lips. The human animatedly followed suit. How easy obtaining surrender—gaining their lives, with but a whispered wish. Only a self-directed thought could stop him. Compelled to do his bidding, humans had none of their own. They were putty, their guided deeds at the whim of the wraith's imagination.

J.W. Garrett has been writing in one form or another since she was a teenager. She currently lives in Florida with her family but loves the mountains of Virginia where she was born. Her writings include YA fantasy as well as short stories. Since completing Remeon's Quest-Earth Year 1930, the prequel in her YA fantasy series, Realms of Chaos, she has been hard at work on the next in the series, scheduled to release June 2020. When she's not hanging out with her characters, her favourite activities are reading, running and spending time with family.
Website: www.jwgarrett.com
BHC Press: www.bhcpress.com/Author_JW_Garrett.html

Human Pizza
by C.L. Williams

I work at a pizza shop and I have a secret no one else knows; I'm a cannibal. I love the taste of human flesh.

Unfortunately, people look down at that. I did, however, find a book of curses that allows me to put a curse on people to make them look like food while I chow down. In my case, I make them look like pizza and no one suspects a thing. I turn people into pizzas; I eat what I need to, then I sell the others.

No one knows the meal of the day is human pizza.

C.L. Williams *is an independent author from central Virginia. He has written eight poetry books, four novellas, one novel, and a contributor to multiple anthologies, with the most recent appearance being an all-ages anthology titled Temoli from Thazbook. His most recent poetry book, The Paradox Complex, features the poem "Sad Crying Clown" that is now a video on YouTube directed by Matthew Mark Hunter of MMH Productions. C.L. Williams is currently working on his first sci-fi book, an all-ages book titled Novo: Away from Earth. When not writing, C.L. Williams is reading and sharing the work of other independent authors.*
Facebook: writer434
Twitter: @writer_434

Deadland Spirits
by Pamela Jeffs

I was born of desert sunlight and the blistering western winds. A Deadland spirit. But this existence is not enough. I can ride the currents of air that rise off these ancient sands, but I have no voice with which to speak.

And such a thing I desire.

So, I hunt—hunt for body parts that can be sewn together to gift me speech.

My tastes are specific. I take the scaled-skinned huntsmen that dwell in these lands. I harvest the finest of them—the strong, the clever, the quick-witted. And I covet most, those with voices best for singing.

Pamela Jeffs is a speculative fiction author living in Queensland, Australia with her husband and two daughters. She is a member of the Queensland Writers' Centre and has had numerous short fiction pieces published in recent national and international anthologies. In 2017 and again in 2018, Pamela was nominated for an Australian Aurealis Award in the category of 'Best Science Fiction Short Story'. Her debut collection titled 'Red Hour and Other Strange Tales' was released in March 2018.
Website: www.pamelajeffs.com
Facebook: pamelajeffsauthor

Protect the Baby
by Stephen Herczeg

The full moon shone bright.

Dad sat on the swing-chair, shotgun in his lap.

"Let 'em come tonight. I'll protect the chickens, you protect the baby."

An eerie howl broke from the gloom.

Dad cocked the hammers on the gun.

I ducked back inside.

The baby was sound asleep in her crib. The windows were locked. A shaft of moonlight lanced into the room.

A *boom* at the front of the house. I raced onto the porch. Dad disappeared into the darkness.

A tinkling of glass, a short high-pitched cry.

I ran to the nursery.

The crib was empty.

"Nooooooooooooooooooooooooooo."

Stephen Herczeg is an IT Geek based in Canberra Australia. He has been writing for over twenty years and has completed a couple of dodgy novels, sixteen feature length screenplays and numerous short stories and scripts. His horror work has featured in Sproutlings, Hells Bells, Below the Stairs, Trickster's Treats #1 and #2, Shades of Santa, Behind the Mask, Beyond the Infinite; The Body Horror Book, Anemone Enemy, Petrified Punks and Beginnings. He has also had numerous Sherlock Holmes stories published through the Belanger Books - Sherlock Holmes anthologies.

Paper Or...
by A.L. King

Plastic? Are they *still* plastic? Were they *ever*?

Whatever their anatomy or origin, the monsters mounted a Trojan-like coup. Shoppers carried them inside and stored them—for later use—inside cabinets and drawers with their balled-up brethren.

Then B-Day arrived. No, not BIRTHDAY! It means BAG DAY now.

They were finished being used to pick up dog shit during walks or to provide an extra layer around breakables. They burst forth and overtook Earth. They floated around like airborne jellyfish and adhered to human skin as they fed.

If we could go back, surely we would answer differently.

"Paper, please."

A.L. King is an author of horror, fantasy, science fiction, and poetry. As an avid fan of dark subjects from an early age, his first influences included R.L. Stine, Edgar Allan Poe, and Stephen King. Later stylistic inspirations came from foreign horror films and media, particularly Japanese. He is a graduate of West Liberty University, has dabbled in journalism, and is actively involved in his community. Although his creativity leans toward darker genres, he has even written a children's book titled "Leif's First Fall." He was raised in the town of Sistersville, West Virginia, which he still proudly calls home.

Little Jo's First Time
by Cindy O'Quinn

Regardless of what time of day the farmer went to the barn for chores, the little one always trailed close behind. "Grab the special pail, Little Jo."

Josephine stood on the chair and reached up to retrieve the pail from the hook. "Look, I don't have to stand on my tippy-toes anymore."

Smiling, the farmer looked back at her. "Before long, you'll be eight years old."

"Come on, Daddy, you know I'm eight today."

Today was special. For the first time, Little Jo would be in charge of bleeding the human for their celebration, and her mouth watered in anticipation.

Cindy O'Quinn is an Appalachian writer who grew up in the mountains of West Virginia. Cindy is the author of _Dark Cloud on Naked Creek_, and the dark poetry collection, _Return to Graveyard Dust_, which made it to the 2017 HWA Bram Stoker preliminary ballot. Her work has been published or is forthcoming in Twisted Book of Shadows, the HWA Poetry Showcase Vol. V, Nothing's Sacred Vol. 4 & 5, Rag Queen Periodical, Moonchild Magazine, Sanitarium Magazine, and others.
Twitter: @COQuinnWrites
Facebook: CindyOQuinnWriter

The Ball
by Ximena Escobar

Leda stretched her neck, entering the frame of the rear-view mirror. Her metallic make-up lustred like moondust; purple hues streamed down her curls and onto her bare shoulders.

She sat back, looking at the streetlamps bypassing them in the fog.

"I didn't realise it was so far out," she said, feeling the driver's gaze slide furtively onto her cleavage.

"It'll be worth it, Miss Spade," he said.

She caressed the lustrous envelope with her thumb, looking at her name in beautiful calligraphy.

"Are we there yet?" she asked.

The mirror didn't reflect the long white fangs appearing in his smile.

Ximena Escobar is an emerging author of literary fiction and poetry. Originally from Chile, she is the author of a translation into Spanish of the Broadway Musical "The Wizard of Oz", and of an original adaptation of the same, "Navidad en Oz". Clarendon House Publications published her first short story in the UK, "The Persistence of Memory", and Literally Stories her first online publication with "The Green Light". She has since had several acceptances from other publishers and is working very hard exploring new exciting avenues in her writing.
She lives in Nottingham with her family.
Facebook: Ximenautora

Date Night
by Rowanne S. Carberry

Joe looks down at his hands, his fingers starting to elongate. Not now, please not now. Looking at his date he tries to think of an excuse to bail. Nothing comes to mind.

"I need to go the toilet," Joe blurts out.

Keeping his hands from view, Joe runs to the back and through a fire exit.

Hair starts sprouting and his spine bends, screams of pain turning into a howl.

"Joe?" His ears prick up and his nose quivers.

Wolf eyes staring at his date, he pounces, his claws slicing into her before she has the chance to scream.

Rowanne S. Carberry was born in England in 1990, where she stills lives now with her cat Wolverine. Rowanne has always loved writing, and her first poem was published at the age of 15, but her ambition has always been to help people. Rowanne studied at the University of Sunderland where she completed combined honours of Psychology with Drama. Rowanne writes to offer others an escape. Although Rowanne writes in varied genres each story or poem she writes will often have a darkness to it, which helped coin her brand, Poisoned Quill Writing – Wicked words from a poisoned quill.
Facebook: PoisonedQuillWriting
Instagram: @poisoned_quill_writing

Ven's Refuge
by Austin P. Sheehan

Everyone needs a shelter. A place they can drop their masks, where they can be alone.

Ven had such a place. As he pressed his forehead against the cool rock, his stress and fear drained away. Not even the voices that tormented him could reach Ven here.

Still, something was wrong. His face felt wet and sticky. Heart racing, he touched his face and raised his hand into the moonlight. Dark blood covered his hands, dripping down his arms. *Not again.* As he fell to his knees, severing the contact with the stone, the laughter of those terrible voices returned.

Austin P. Sheehan is a writer of speculative fiction, a lover of language, literature and '90s TV. Armed with a psychology degree, he went into the world to study humanity, and now prefers the company of his wife and their greyhounds. He grew up in the valleys of Victoria's high country, and despite living in Melbourne, always feels at home amongst the mountains. You'll often find mountains in his stories, whether they're sci-fi, fantasy or alternative history.
Website: austinpsheehan.com
Twitter: @AustinPSheehan

A Prayer
by K.T. Tate

Make me a monster. Let this mask become my face. Let my teeth grow and my eyes glow. Shift my form. Twist my bones and make me a predator. Make the shadows my cloak, my voice a haunting howl. Exchange these hands for talons, perfect to rend and tear.

Take all my pain; let it be kindling on the fire of my incandescent rage. My soul will know justice, bloody and raw. He will scream as I have screamed, suffer as I have suffered. They will know what he did. Let the stories of his shredded corpse be a warning.

K.T. Tate lives in Cambridgeshire in the UK. She writes mainly weird fiction, cosmic horror and strange monster stories.
Website: eldritchhollow.wordpress.com
Tumblr: eldritch-hollow.tumblr.com

The Pearl Diver
by J.M. Meyer

The pearl diver reaches the surface and blows out her traditional whistling breath, characteristic of the ama. Akina, 78, decides this will be her last dive. She places her bag with the sandy pearls on the deck of the boat that tethers her to life. Akina swiftly removes her symbolled headscarf, which has warded off the evils of the deep since 13. Her ama sisters scream pulling at the rope as Akina dives, down, down. She kisses then drops her knife after cutting the taut rope, swimming to demons who have been beckoning her with what she believes is love.

J.M. Meyer is writer, artist and small business owner living in New York., where she received her master's degree from Teacher's College, Columbia University. Jacqueline loves the science fiction and horror genres. Reading Ray Bradbury was a mind-blowing experience for her in 8th grade. Alfred Hitchcock and Rod Serling were the horror heroes of her youth. Mercedes M. Yardley is her current horror writing hero. Jacqueline also enjoys the company of her husband Bruce and their three children, Julia, Emma and Lauren. Jacqueline's mantra: The only time it's too late to try something new is when you are dead.
Website: jmoranmeyer.net
Twitter: @moran_meyer

A Moment Like Eternity
by Ximena Escobar

The impact of my fist upon her grin unfolds like a reverberation but, as such, it vanishes. I can't reach it. I chase it, riding the inertia of my wheel of dissatisfaction, but it's the nightmare descending; her giggles reaching me. Daddy, wake up, Daddy.

It's me I want to destroy. My guilt wants to destroy me; centre of my self-loathing blackhole covering my mouth. I can't breathe for an eternal second.

I cannot tell you, but I love you, baby. Forgive me. I cannot see the world through your beautiful eyes. I can't remember me. Dissolved under the fist.

Ximena Escobar is an emerging author of literary fiction and poetry. Originally from Chile, she is the author of a translation into Spanish of the Broadway Musical "The Wizard of Oz", and of an original adaptation of the same, "Navidad en Oz". Clarendon House Publications published her first short story in the UK, "The Persistence of Memory", and Literally Stories her first online publication with "The Green Light". She has since had several acceptances from other publishers and is working very hard exploring new exciting avenues in her writing.
She lives in Nottingham with her family.
Facebook: Ximenautora

Child Care
by Rickey Rivers Jr.

My wife had to pry the knife out of my hand. She was screaming. She was crying.

I reassured. It had to be done.

She understood. Yet we both knew that the image would persistently haunt.

A child is supposed to be a blessing. Yet our child was born woolly with many teeth. We tried our best to love it.

Eventually it developed an appetite, an appetite for something in particular. Breast feeding was inadequate. My wife has the marks.

We started small, feeding it mice, but it couldn't satisfy the animalistic hunger.

What I did had to be done.

Rickey Rivers Jr. was born and raised in Alabama. He is a writer and cancer survivor. He likes a lot of stuff. You don't care about the details. He has been previously published in Fabula Argentea, ARTPOST magazine, the anthology Chronos, Enchanted Conversations Magazine, (among other publications).
Twitter: @storiesyoumight

Jason
by Vickie J. Litten

My nephew came to stay with us. My sister couldn't handle him.

One evening, he fell asleep in front of the television. As I walked past him, I noticed his eyes were half open. I bent down to check if he was awake, and when I looked into those eyes, a cold chill grasped my chest and I couldn't breathe for a second. The eyes looking at me, weren't his eyes.

I knew at that moment he wasn't a troubled kid, he was possessed by something evil. We put him on a bus and sent him back to his mother.

Vickie J. Litten *lives in South Florida with her husband, two sons, three grandchildren, her deaf dog and Savannah cat. She loves to write, and also enjoys art, photography, cooking and gardening.*

Sansara
by Oleg Hasanov

Karma didn't let him reach nirvana, and he found himself swimming comfortably in the amniotic fluids. But that was alright. Soon he would be born again. He liked mortal life and would be happy to live one more.

Something moved beside him. Something alive. A brother or a sister. Good. He wouldn't be so lonely in the new life. Something moved again. Closer. It touched him. He turned lovingly as dozens of teeth, sharp like awls, pierced his flesh and began tearing, cutting and grinding it. He opened his mouth in a silent scream.

His little brother sharks were hungry.

Oleg Hasanov is a writer and translator based in Russia. He lives in the city of Chelyabinsk, where men are so tough that they light cigarettes off meteorites. He mainly writes fiction in English.

Experimentation
by Joel R. Hunt

Gomez was still combing the office for evidence when Blaire emerged from the basement, pale faced and shaking.

"The professor didn't kill them," he mumbled.

"What do you mean?" asked Gomez, "Our witnesses, the emails, the CCTV…it all points here."

Blaire shook his head, numb. Gomez strode past her colleague and descended the basement steps. She peered through darkness, past vials and cages and surgical tools, until a gurgling sound caught her attention. On an operating table, she saw a quivering mass of hair, flesh and faces.

Blaire was right.

The professor hadn't killed a single one of them.

Joel R. Hunt is a writer from the UK who dabbles in the darker aspects of life, particularly through horror, science fiction and the supernatural. He has been published here and there (though likely nowhere you've heard of) and hopes to have released his first anthology of short stories later this year.
Twitter: @JoelRHunt1
Reddit: JRHEvilInc

A Doggy's Heart
by Alanna Robertson-Webb

"Good doggy! Please don't eat me...I'm sure you have a good heart..."

Her tear-filled whimpers were music to my ears. She was right, there was a good heart inside of me, but it was just a backup in case my current ticker broke down. I growled with laughter, and I relished ripping the flesh off the stupid human who didn't realise the irony of her own words.

All were animals have multiple organs, and we can even eat the extras if food runs out. Too bad for her I was starving, or I might have thought about sparing her life.

Alanna Robertson-Webb is a sales support member by day, and a writer and editor by night. She loves VT, and lives in NY. She has been writing since she was five years old, and writing well since she was seventeen years old. She lives with a fiance and a cat, both of whom take up most of her bed space. She loves to L.A.R.P., and one day she aspired to write a horrifyingly fantastic novel. Her short horror stories have been published before, but she still enjoys remaining mysterious.
Reddit: MythologyLovesHorror

As Others See Us
by John H. Dromey

"Why on Earth did you choose Germany for your meeting with the Olympian ambassador?"

"For practical reasons. Our encounter will be '*unter vier Augen.*' I plan to wear sunglasses with a reflective coating."

"You're linguistically-challenged, aren't you?"

"Maybe. Is there a problem?"

"Yes. In the English language 'four eyes' is slang for wearing glasses. In German, 'under four eyes' means in private—only two eyes per participant in the conversation. Dark glasses are definitely out. You'll need to keep ninety-eight of your eyes closed at all times during the meeting."

It isn't easy being a bug-eyed monster from outer space.

First published in *Little Stories for the Smallest Room* by KnightWatch Press, 2012

John H. Dromey was born in northeast Missouri, USA. He enjoys reading—mysteries in particular—and writing in a variety of genres. He's had short fiction published in Alfred Hitchcock's Mystery Magazine, Martian Magazine, Stupefying Stories Showcase, Thriller Magazine, Unfit Magazine, and elsewhere, as well as in a number of anthologies, including Chilling Horror Short Stories (Flame Tree Publishing, 2015).

The Leviathan
by Sam M. Phillips

The leviathan, a massive snake from the sea, smashes the city apart. Only one thing can save us, and we dread it almost as much as the leviathan.

A colossal robot, the protector of the city, rises from a portal. It runs forward, crushing thousands underfoot.

The two goliaths collide with a sound like thunder. We huddle in fear as everything is destroyed in their titanic struggle.

When the battle is over, and the leviathan lies dead, we emerge, many thousands killed, the city destroyed. Now we must rebuild, but at least there is plenty of snake meat to eat.

Sam M. Phillips is the co-founder of Zombie Pirate Publishing, producing short story anthologies and helping emerging writers. His own work has appeared in dozens of anthologies and magazines such as Full Moon Slaughter 2, 13 Bites Volumes IV and V, Rejected for Content 6, and Dastaan World Magazine. He lives in the green valleys of northern New South Wales, Australia, and enjoys reading, walking, and playing drums in the death metal band Decryptus.
Website: zombiepiratepublishing.com
Blog: bigconfusingwords.wordpress.com

Trophy Hunting
by Stuart Conover

Pain tore through Angela's body.

Flesh and bone rearranged themselves.

She had blacked out from her first change.

Now she didn't even flinch.

She shook off.

Flexed.

Stretched her back.

Tail wagging as heightened senses kicked in.

Dangers lurked in the forest for a wild creature.

A shifter wasn't wild.

Sniffing the air, she caught the scent.

Sprinting, it wasn't long until she found her pray.

Slow.

Stupid.

A killer without honour.

She pounced.

A crack of thunder filled the air.

Too late.

She was upon the beast.

Tearing into its throat.

Another worthless trophy hunter's carcass for the pile.

Stuart Conover is a father, husband, rescue dog owner, published author, blogger, journalist, horror enthusiast, comic book geek, science fiction junkie, and IT professional. With all of that to cram in daily, we have no idea if or when he sleeps or how he gets writing done! (We suspect it has to do with having evil clones.) Stuart is a Chicago native and runs the author resource Horror Tree.

Halloween Treats
by R.G. Halstead

It had been a good night. Plenty to eat, delivered right to the door—fresh was always best.

But their oven was acting up. Some of the meat wasn't cooked completely. Hot, yes, but a bit raw in places.

Still yummy, though.

The elderly Nortons had sliced up their unsuspecting prey tonight and roasted their dinner. They didn't feel guilty. They didn't feel hungry anymore.

"Well, dear," Ed said to his wife. "We carved up and ate all those Halloween trick-or-treaters. What should we do with their costumes? And candy?"

"Sell them. Use the money to buy a new oven."

R.G. Halstead, a 63-year-old, takes to writing late in his life. Influences? Those old Alfred Hitchcock Mystery Magazines from the late 1950s and the 1960s with the great twisty endings. Love them.

Mr Sandman, Bring Me a Scream
by Terry Miller

The Sandman never came last night, nor the night before. Kiera guzzled coffee this morning just to make it through work, barely functioning.

One more night of hell. Kiera skipped work. She didn't even care. They can fire me, she thought. She just wished she could get a few hours' sleep.

It was so warm under the covers. Kiera lay snug. Her mind was drifting. Above her, a shadowy figure lurched. Its jaws opened wide, a fine, salty grain poured down from its gaping mouth. Her eyes burned as she clawed at them relentlessly, screaming. Finally, the Sandman had come.

Terry Miller is an author and 2017 Rhysling Award-nominated poet residing in Portsmouth, OH, USA. He has self-published a dark poetry collection on Amazon and one short story to date. His work has also appeared in Sanitarium, Devolution Z, Jitter Press, Poetry Quarterly, O Unholy Night in Deathlehem, and the 2017 Rhysling Anthology from the Science Fiction and Fantasy Poetry Association.
Facebook: tmiller2015

The Waygrim
by Cecelia Hopkins-Drewer

"Unlike a regular predator, the waygrim doesn't kill because it is hungry," the Professor said. "And unlike the werewolf who is driven into a frenzy by the full moon, it is aware of its actions. The waygrim kills because it can. It is cold hearted, absolute cruelty."

The students shuddered at this dramatic pronouncement. All except one, who calmly stood up and transformed into a black dog.

"Thanks for the lesson, Professor," he said. "It has been most informative. Now I must follow my nature!"

The class screamed as the waygrim slashed the throat of the lecturer with his teeth.

Cecelia Hopkins-Drewer *is a speculative fiction writer, poet and scholar, who lives in Adelaide, South Australia. She has also written a Masters paper on H.P. Lovecraft, and a teenage vampire series that commences with "Mystic Evermore". Her science fiction poetry has been published in "The Mentor" a fanzine edited by Ron Clarke.*
Amazon: amazon.com/Cecelia-Hopkins-Drewer/e/B071G968NM

Terror in the Deep
by Zoey Xolton

Captain Argent took the helm, gripping tight with white knuckles as the sea assaulted the *Queen Bess*. There was a storm coming, that much was evident, but there was something else…the way the sea boiled and rolled.

He'd never seen its like before.

Before he could ponder the chaos further, the mast came crashing down. He dived out of the way, just in time. His mast and several of his men disappeared beneath the waves, pulled to Davy Jones' locker by tentacles the size of tree trunks.

"The Kraken!" he bellowed into the wind. There could be no doubt.

Zoey Xolton is an Australian Speculative Fiction writer, primarily of Dark Fantasy, Paranormal Romance and Horror. She is also a proud mother of two and is married to her soul mate. Outside of her family, writing is her greatest passion. She is especially fond of short fiction and is working on releasing her own themed collections in future.
Website: www.zoeyxolton.com

The Sneering Guest
by Gregg Cunningham

I'd recognise that Smirk anywhere.

He was the one that ransacked my garden, stole all my berries, and ate all my birdseed. When you see that Smirk, you know there is going to be trouble

Oh, these little fellas are not your garden variety Smirk, oh no.

What happens is these little bags of teeth get a hankering for all things juicy, first the berries, then the frightened pets trapped in their cages at the bottom of the garden.

Once that happens, Smirks turn into Sneers, and when Sneers get a whiff of fear, that's when things turn really nasty.

Gregg Cunningham *48, short story writer who has had to pick up his game since stumbling into facebook writer's groups. He has stories published by 559 Publishing in in 13 Bites volume 3,4,5, Plan 9 from Outer space, Other Realms, Heard It on The Radio, 559 Ways to Die, short stories publishing by Zombie Pirate Publishing in Relationship add Vice, Full Metal Horror, Phuket Tattoo, World War four and Flash Fiction Addiction (flash) with Zombie Pirate Publishing, and also in Daastan Magazine Chapter 11 and Brian,Rich and the Wardrobe.*
Amazon: www.amazon.com/-/e/B016OTHX0K

You
by Cecelia Hopkins-Drewer

You approach the kitchen cupboard and open the door. You never really believe in closet monsters, but one is there. It isn't vague and dark like the shadow of the cups; it is small and has many teeth. Like a flying gremlin, or is it Grimlin?

The Grimlin is fast; it takes a bite out of your nose and zooms out of the cupboard into the room. You look around for a weapon. Grab the fly spray and your hardcover cookbook.

You swat it too late. Noses don't grow back, and the Grimlin just spat burning acid in your eye.

Cecelia Hopkins-Drewer is a speculative fiction writer, poet and scholar, who lives in Adelaide, South Australia. She has also written a Masters paper on H.P. Lovecraft, and a teenage vampire series that commences with "Mystic Evermore". Her science fiction poetry has been published in "The Mentor" a fanzine edited by Ron Clarke.
Amazon: amazon.com/Cecelia-Hopkins-Drewer/e/B071G968NM

Incoming!
by Bob Adder

"Incoming!"

'Incoming' was very wrong. 'Incoming' was about five minutes too late.

It stood there in front of them. Blood dripping from its rotting maw, chunks of flesh stuck in its decaying teeth. Its back arched into a slumped walk, slowly growing faster the closer it got, limbs flying towards them as if they were no longer attached to its body.

Solar stood there, frozen, as it moved inches from her face.

A gun shot fired and *It* slumped over in front of her.

"Are you trying to die?" Jackson yelled, putting his gun away. "It would have eaten you."

***Bob Adder** is an aspiring author and superhero geek from Melbourne, Australia.*

Spring-Heeled Jack
by David Bowmore

Mother warned me. I didn't listen.

She said, "Be a good girl or Spring-Heeled Jack will have ya. Ain't no one lives after seeing his ugly fizog, and his flashing tail. They say he runs you through with a red hot poker wot he stole from under the devil's nose."

"If no one lives, how come they know so much about him?"

"Never you mind. Just don't try earning a shilling in no back ally. Hear me?"

"Yes, Mum."

I saw him springing over iron railings and scaling the sides of houses, as he left me dying in the filth.

David Bowmore has lived here, there and everywhere, but now lives in Yorkshire with his wonderful wife and a small white poodle. He has worn many hats in his time; head chef, teacher and landscape gardener. His first collection of short stories 'The Magic of Deben Market' is available from Clarendon House.
Website: davidbowmore.co.uk
Facebook: davidbowmoreauthor

There Goes the Neighbourhood
by Morgan Chalfant

Her morning jog through the neighbourhood was Clover's most important ritual.

Mr. Swoford waved, starting his mower. She smiled and waved back.

"Hi!" she said, as Kerry and Lorenzo jogged past her.

A few more yards and Clover stepped inside her house. She stretched and went directly to the basement.

Chains jingled. Muffled moans.

"Morning, Leslie!" She grinned at the bloodied woman dangling from the rafters. "Well, my morning workout is done! Let's start yours!"

Clover was wrong; *this* was her most important morning ritual. Clover picked up her sacrificial blade from the workbench and blew the woman a kiss.

Morgan Chalfant is a native of Hill City, Kansas. He received a Bachelor's degree in writing and a Master's degree in literature from Fort Hays State University. His short story, "The Steel Music Box" appeared in the horror anthology, Dark and Evil. Another of his stories, "Little Neon" will be appearing in the forthcoming anthology, Crash Code.
Facebook: themorgancchalfant

No Such Thing as Monsters
by Lyndsey Ellis-Holloway

There's no such thing as monsters.

There's no such thing.

That's what they tell you as a kid.

I used to believe them. But as I got older, I realised it was just a convenient lie to make me go to bed.

The older you get, the more you understand; there are plenty of monsters. Whether you see them as such depends on where you're standing on the food chain.

I used to be the victim you see; my mum was my monster.

Now? She's gone…I took her place.

Her blood is on my hands.

I'm the monster now.

Lyndsey Ellis-Holloway is a writer from Knaresborough, UK. She writes fantasy, sci-fi, horror and dystopian stories, focussing on compelling characters and layering in myth and legend at every opportunity. When she's not writing she spends time with her husband, her dogs and her friends enjoying activities such a walking, movies, conventions and of course writing for fun as well!

Catastrophe
by Serena Jayne

Shannon wrestled the Corgi-sized black cat from its carrier and dropped it on Aunt Janet's casket. "Steal her soul and I'll give you cream."

The cat scampered into the adjacent parlour and leapt onto the chest of the corpse on display.

Shannon's heart sank. "Bad Sith kitty."

She didn't know if kitty was fairy or demon, but she didn't pay to have the thing overnighted from Scotland to Chicago to ruin the wrong person's afterlife. "*Aunt Janet*'s who disinherited me—not that *stiff*!"

With a flick of its tail, the beast darted past the stunned funeral director into the night.

Serena Jayne is a graduate of Seton Hill University's Writing Popular Fiction MFA Program. Her short fiction and poetry can be found in Switchblade Magazine, the Drabble, Crack the Spine Literary Magazine, 101 Fiction, the Oddville Press, and other publications.
Website: www.serenajayne.com
Twitter: @SJ_Writer

The Man Eating Lobster
by Scott Hughes

"See the six-foot man eating lobster!" exclaimed the carnival barker. "Only a dollar!"

Taylor and Anthony, tipsy on watered-down beer, stopped at the ratty sideshow tent.

"Seen this before," Taylor muttered. "Just some dude eating a lobster."

"Wanna bet?" said Anthony. "Ten bucks says it ain't. It's something animatronical."

They shook on it, then paid the grinning barker. Inside, blinking Christmas lights overhead illuminated an enormous muddy aquarium.

Anthony tapped the glass. "Pay up!"

As Taylor dug in his pocket for a tenner, two mottled brown claws as big as the men's torsos hauled them screaming into the murky water.

Scott Hughes's fiction, poetry, and essays have appeared in such publications as *Crazyhorse*, *One Sentence Poems*, *Deep Magic*, *Redheaded Stepchild*, *Entropy*, and *Strange Horizons*. He is the Division Head of English at Central Georgia Technical College. His horror short story collection, *The Last Book You'll Ever Read*, is forthcoming from Weasel Press in 2019, and his poetry collection, *The Universe You Swallowed Whole*, is forthcoming from Finishing Line Press.
Website: writescott.com

One Case Too Many
by Roxanne Dent

When P.I. Li woke up, she lay in a coffin, a body on top of her.

Panicked, Li shoved the body to one side and strained to lift the heavy lid. It didn't budge.

Her memory began to return. Julia hired her to find her fiancé, Bryce.

A spade clattered above. The coffin lid rose. Li breathed in mouthfuls of cool night air.

Julia helped her out.

"What happened?"

"I drugged you and placed you there."

Li stared. "Why?

"For him."

Li turned.

Bryce pulled her close. She screamed as he dug his fangs deep into her neck and drank.

Roxanne Dent has sold nine novels and dozens of short stories in a variety of genres including Paranormal Fantasy, Regency, Mystery, Horror and YA. She has also co-authored short stories and plays with her sister, Karen Dent. Member of New England Horror Writers, The Fiction Writers Guild, Berlin Writers Group, Essex Writers and Artists Group.

For Sale: One Owner
by Peter J. Foote

"$50 bucks? That seems too good to be true," Larry says as he kicks the dirt bike's tire.

"Well, I just want her to have a good home," the old man says as Larry pulls out his wallet.

"Whoa there! You can't take her without a test run. The trail is a little rough, but she can probably do it on her own." The old man laughs.

Larry roars away trailing blue smoke. Moments later, a cry echoes up the trail and the bike returns alone, putting along, and parks beside the old man.

"We got another one, old girl."

Peter J. Foote is a bestselling speculative fiction writer from Nova Scotia. Outside of writing, he runs a used bookstore specialising in fantasy & sci-fi, cosplays, and alternates between red wine and coffee as the mood demands. His short stories can be found in both print and in ebook form, with his story "Sea Monkeys" winning the inaugural "Engen Books/Kit Sora, Flash Fiction/Flash Photography" contest in March of 2018. As the founder of the group "Genre Writers of Atlantic Canada", Peter believes that the writing community is stronger when it works together.
Twitter: @PeterJFoote1
Website: peterjfooteauthor.wordpress.com

Witch at the Stake
by E.L. Giles

"Witch! Witch! Witch!" they yell in a singular voice.

I am taken across the gathering of villagers toward the tree-shrouded hill.

"Witch at the stake!" they chant, the dissonant melody sending tremors of fear as I am roped against the stiff wooden stake.

"What was my crime but to love the stone-hearted man and defy his puritan morality?" I ask.

Eyes full of scorn, they respond, "Burn! Burn! Burn!"

The flames elevate like their infectious hate under the scorching summer sun.

"I curse you all for generations! And the children of your children, at thirty-three, will burn at the stake."

E.L. Giles is a dreamer, passionate about art, a restless worker and a bit of a weird human. He started his artistic journey as a music composer until the need to put his thoughts and stories down on paper grew too strong for him to resist it any longer. He lives in the French Province of Quebec, Canada, with his girlfriend and two boys.
Facebook: elgilesauthor
Website: www.elgilesauthor.com

I Rest My Case
by Glenn R. Wilson

"Your Honour, I appeal to the court on behalf of my client—" It was here that Mr. Overpriced extended his hand in my direction. "—who has the misfortune of suffering the prejudice of this court—" Now, it was the judge's turn to hold up his hand and ask for a verdict.

Before the gangly juror cleared his throat to speak the word I knew was coming, I assessed the situation and figured I had nothing to lose…

The judge was the last one I tried. A little greasy, but sweet. Not as tough as my lawyer. Better than the jury.

Glenn R. Wilson has come full circle. Making a point to mature, like fine wine, before diving head-first into his long list of writing projects, he's approaching them with a plan. That strategy is to build with one brick at a time. He's accumulated a few bricks already and is adding more. Over time, with persistence and determination, he'll have a home. But for now, a solid foundation is the goal. Please, enjoy the process with him.

Frenzy
by Jem McCusker

His fists beat a drum, they pounded then they clawed, no match for my strength, I drank it all.

Warm liquid, hotter than hell, surged through my veins. In a moment of glory, I rejoiced aloud, for angels' blood was now mixed with mine. A chance of a new life, of daylight walks spawned.

I heard them then; the hounds came at a run, hell burning liquid amber in their eyes. I turned to leave, no match for their speed. In a frenzy, fangs pierced my flesh, tearing limbs. I still had a chance if they left me in bits.

Jem McCusker is a middle grade fiction author, living near Brisbane with her two sons and husband. Her first book Stone Guardians the Rise of Eden was released in 2018 and she is working on the sequel. She is releasing a Novella for the Four Quills writing group, A Storm of Wind and Rain series in July, 2019. She longs to be a full-time author, won't wear yellow and loves rabbits. Follow Jem on Twitter, Facebook and Instagram. Details on her website.
Website: www.jemmccusker.com

Strzyga
by Jacek Wilkos

Paralyzed by fear, the priest watched a woman tearing people apart with her bare hands, one by one. When the screams subsided, he understood it was his turn. He dropped to his knees and folded his hands.

Prayers will not save your wretched life. The murderess entered the presbytery. Blood dripped from her hands and lips.

"Die! Begone, you soulless demon!" the priest shouted, waving his cross.

Soulless? But I have a soul, and I even had two until you took one away from me. And now I will take yours.

The creature smiled, revealing two rows of sharp teeth.

Jacek Wilkos is an engineer from Poland. He lives with his wife and daughter in a beautiful city of Cracow. He writes mostly horror drabbles. His fiction in Polish can be read on Szortal, Niedobre literki, Horror Online. Lately he started translating his stories into English with the hope of publishing them.
Facebook: Jacek.W.Wilkos

The Shed
by C.L. Williams

Johnny wakes up tied to a table in the shed. The last thing he saw before losing consciousness, a person in a clown mask, is standing over him.

"It's time to get what you deserve," the voice whispers in Johnny's ear.

Johnny starts screaming as the person removes the clown mask. The face behind the clown mask is not human. The demonic-looking entity is hungry for flesh and Johnny happens to be still enough for it to consider Johnny its next feast. Johnny tries to scream, but it's of no use as he is now the meal to this monster.

C.L. Williams is an independent author from central Virginia. He has written eight poetry books, four novellas, one novel, and a contributor to multiple anthologies, with the most recent appearance being an all-ages anthology titled Temoli from Thazbook. His most recent poetry book, The Paradox Complex, features the poem "Sad Crying Clown" that is now a video on YouTube directed by Matthew Mark Hunter of MMH Productions. C.L. Williams is currently working on his first sci-fi book, an all-ages book titled Novo: Away from Earth. When not writing, C.L. Williams is reading and sharing the work of other independent authors.
Facebook: writer434
Twitter: @writer_434

'Til Death Do Us Part
by D.M. Burdett

I awoke, my head heavy and my vision blurred into a thousand fractured pieces of darkness.

I felt no pain.

Vague memories of the monster fluttered at the periphery of my consciousness, and I moved my eyes to search for him in the gloom. I saw him eating.

I felt no fear.

The monster's prey looked at me with dead eyes. A hazy memory of those now-grey eyes—bright and alive, and filled with love—floated to the surface but was snuffed out by a white-hot compulsion that blinded my thoughts forever.

I crawled over to share my maker's meal.

D.M. Burdett initially roamed as an army brat, but now lives in Australia where she spends her days avoiding drop bears and killer spiders. She has published a Sci-Fi series, has short stories in various anthologies, and has published two children's series. She is currently working on the first book in a dystopian series.
Website: www.dmburdett.com
Facebook: DMBurdett

Man of Straw
by David Bowmore

He had stood watch over the barren field for hundreds of years.

Crows had come and gone. They had mostly come to peck at his innards.

The girl was alone, lost on the old yellow road, itself lost under a sea of moss and debris.

He didn't like what was about to happen, but he needed to rest. After all, he was only a straw-man.

She reminded him of the other one, and she had a dog too.

The trick was easy; she was so willing to believe his clever lies.

Now, she could scare the crows for a while.

David Bowmore has lived here, there and everywhere, but now lives in Yorkshire with his wonderful wife and a small white poodle. He has worn many hats in his time; head chef, teacher and landscape gardener. His first collection of short stories 'The Magic of Deben Market' is available from Clarendon House.
Website: davidbowmore.co.uk
Facebook: davidbowmoreauthor

The Sluagh
by Raven Corinn Carluk

Kevin hallucinated as he died. He pointed at the window, hand shaking. "They're here." I looked to the window to humour him.

Claws screeched against glass, hollow faces peered around the edges, and glowing eyes cast ethereal light. They shifted with each gust, their voices the shrieks of the wind.

The fairy host poured inside as if the glass didn't exist. I shot to my feet as they swarmed Kevin, too frightened to do anything. Even when they ripped his screaming soul from his body, I could do nothing.

They left as quickly. I understood why Gram covered west-facing windows.

Raven Corinn Carluk is an indie author of dark fantasy and paranormal romance.
Website: RavenCorinnCarluk.Blogspot.Com

A Taste So Sweet
by A.R. Johnston

The taste was so sweet. Or what he remembered sweet to be. He didn't remember that much anymore. It was frustrating, it actually made him angry not being able to have coherent thoughts that made sense. He growled, pulled and tore into the meat of what he was eating, shoving it into his mouth with abandon.

The more he ate the more coherent his thoughts became. He remembered. He paused in his eating to look at the grey matter that was like slimy sponge in his fingers. Terror rose within him. His family was strewn out before him.

He screamed.

A.R. Johnston is a small-town girl from Nova Scotia, Canada. Her style of writing is considered Urban Fantasy. Her first major publication is part of an anthology called First Love and she has several more titles lined up. She is a lover of coffee, good tv shows, horror flicks, and reader of books. She pretends to be a writer when real life doesn't get in the way. Pesky full-time job and adulting!

Form-a-Fiend
by Shawn M. Klimek

"Welcome to the Form-a-Fiend Workshop," said the proprietor, waving me towards the first station. "Here's where you choose your fiend's skin. Will it be intimidating, relatable or insidious?"

"Something that could jump out of a closet," I said.

"Not a whiskey bottle?"

"A closet," I insisted.

"Understood," he said. Lifting a sagging armful of slimy leather out of the bin, he carried it to the next station and then attached a hose. "Now what kind of dark emotions will you fill it with?"

"An insatiable, murderous hatred," I said.

"Excellent," he said. A motor hummed, and I began to deflate.

Shawn M. Klimek is the middle child of seven creative siblings, a globetrotting, U.S. military spouse, an internationally best-selling short-story writer, a poet, and butler to a Maltese. Almost one hundred of his stories or poems have been published in digital magazines or anthologies, including BHP's Deep Space and the first six books in the Dark Drabbles series.
Website: jotinthedark.blogspot.com
Facebook: shawnmklimekauthor

The Monster Within
by Zoey Xolton

Sarelle.

"Leave me alone."

Sarelle.

Sarelle clutched at her head in frustration and despair. "I said... Leave. Me. Alone!"

You know I can't do that, Sarelle.

"Why can't you just go away and leave me alone?"

Because I am you.

Sarelle rocked back and forth. "No, you're not. No, you're not," she whispered.

Sarelle.

"What?" she choked out.

Look up.

Sarelle slowly lifted her tear-streaked face to stare at her reflection in the dusty mirror.

"I am you," she said to herself. "I am you." Sarelle sobbed. It was true. She was her own monster, and there was no escape.

Zoey Xolton *is an Australian Speculative Fiction writer, primarily of Dark Fantasy, Paranormal Romance and Horror. She is also a proud mother of two and is married to her soul mate. Outside of her family, writing is her greatest passion. She is especially fond of short fiction and is working on releasing her own themed collections in future.*
Website: www.zoeyxolton.com

They Know
by Kyle Harrison

They know everything about you.

There's nothing you can hide.

Once you think you're safe; they'll find you again.

There is nowhere to run, no secret to keep.

They always listen. Even now, even here.

The worst part of all? They look like you or me. They could be your neighbour.

Your brother.

Your father.

Your son.

All we know for sure, is that it takes the male of the species first.

And God help you if you get pregnant. Then they can even hear your secret thoughts.

What little advice I can give is this:

See a man? Run…

Kyle Harrison is a successfully published short story horror novelist and has been in over 6 anthologies and managed 3 anthologies himself. He has also been a project manager for Kickstarters and served as a mentor for other aspiring writers.

Royal Death
by Matthew M. Montelione

Long Island, New York. 1779.

On a cold winter night, a small group of British soldiers found a beaten and bloodied farmer lying in the marshes.

Major Ludlow and his foot soldiers stared at the man.

"Get him to the barracks," the major ordered, "he is on the verge of death."

Later, the weak farmer awoke to the redcoats standing over him. "Where am I?" he hazily asked.

Major Ludlow's dark brown eyes grew intense. His golden gorget shined against the bouncy firelight. "Hell," he calmly said.

Suddenly the major's fangs dropped. The scarlet-clad vampires descended on the terrified man.

Matthew M. Montelione is a horror writer born and raised on Long Island in New York. His stories have been published in Quoth the Raven: A Contemporary Reimagining of the Works of Edgar Allan Poe, Thuggish Itch: Devilish, MONSTERS: A Horror Microfiction Anthology, Eerie Christmas, and other titles. Matthew is also an American Revolution historian who focuses on the local experiences of Loyalists on Long Island. His work on the subject has been published in Long Island History Journal and Journal of the American Revolution. Matthew lives with his wife in New York.
Website: maybeevils.com
Twitter: @maybeevils

The Worst Monster
by Shelly Jarvis

"What is that thing?"

We shake our heads. "We don't know. Scavengers found it in the wreckage. We haven't identified it."

Oba shivers. "We don't like the way it watches us."

We nod, knowing exactly what they mean. "The others think it capable of higher thought functions, but we haven't been able to prove it."

Oba squirms as they watch the creature. "How does it gallop? Four appendages, but only two for moving about. The others are for what, flailing?"

"It does flail a lot," we say.

It has written something again. Strange shapes, indecipherable as we replicate it: HUMAN.

Shelly Jarvis is a speculative fiction author from West Virginia, US. She found a life-long love of sci-fi and fantasy in the 3rd grade when she found Madeleine L'Engle's "A Wrinkle in Time." Shelly is an avid reader, a Whovian, the ideal viewer of dog rescue videos, and undoubtedly Ravenclaw. She currently has two YA sci-fi books available for purchase on Amazon.
Website: www.ShellyJarvis.com

Mr. Latch's Papercut
by Jonathan Inbody

The two-dimensional fiend tore through the man at the counter like tissue paper, then turned and reduced the waitress to ribbons. Screaming families were diced and splattered as the atom-thin beast painted the diner a sickening red. By the door, the salesman smiled. A wounded man crawled toward him begging for help, then screamed as the sharp-edged monster tore into him. Finally, all was silent. Its job done, the creature quickly flattened and leapt back into the briefcase. The salesman quickly closed it and picked it up, then straightened his hat.

"You should have bought what I came to sell."

Jonathan Inbody is a filmmaker, author, and podcaster from Buffalo, New York. He enjoys B-movies, pen and paper RPGs, and New Wave Science Fiction novels. His short story "Dying Feels Like Slowly Sinking" is due to be published in the anthology Deteriorate from Whimsically Dark Publishing. Jon can be heard every other week on his improvisational movie pitch podcast X Meets Y.
Website: xmeetsy.libsyn.com

Giving Thanks
by Stuart Conover

His pale skin glistened in the moonlight.

Jessica was drawn to him.

A moth to a flame.

Heart racing at the thought of being with a Vampyr.

She reached up for his sweet embrace and gasped.

Not in pleasure.

In pain as fangs dug into flesh.

Archibald's kind had been romanticised for decades.

But Bram Stoker knew their nature.

He was not a symbol of love but a hunter.

With the sexualizing of fear, Vampyrs never had it easier.

A flash of fang and Archibald could have anyone he wanted.

At each meal he paused to thank Anne and Stephenie.

Stuart Conover is a father, husband, rescue dog owner, published author, blogger, journalist, horror enthusiast, comic book geek, science fiction junkie, and IT professional. With all of that to cram in daily, we have no idea if or when he sleeps or how he gets writing done! (We suspect it has to do with having evil clones.) Stuart is a Chicago native and runs the author resource Horror Tree.

Back Alley
by Jacek Wilkos

Tim decided to take a shortcut on his way home. Walking through a back alley, he heard a strange groan coming from behind a garbage container. *Maybe somebody needs help,* Tim thought.

He found an old man lying on the pavement. He gently shook his arm.

"Are you okay?"

In response, he heard only a whisper. Tim brought his ear close to the man's lips.

Inner mouthparts sprang and pierced the skull. Injected digestive fluids immediately began to liquify internal organs.

The organism was close to transformation into an imago, and the chrysalis imitating a human effectively lured up food.

Jacek Wilkos is an engineer from Poland. He lives with his wife and daughter in a beautiful city of Cracow. He writes mostly horror drabbles. His fiction in Polish can be read on Szortal, Niedobre literki, Horror Online. Lately he started translating his stories into English with the hope of publishing them.
Facebook: Jacek.W.Wilkos

The Mirror in the Bathroom
by George Nikolopoulos

Officer Jake Delonghi muttered angrily to himself, while shaving. "Another end-of-world prophecy; a mysterious invasion happening today and everyone's going to die. It's in the Potatonic Manuscripts or something. What's worse, the idiots in the Department believe it. We're working double shifts tonight. Is this pathetic or what?"

Looking at the mirror, he saw himself smiling, though he most certainly wasn't. Perplexed, he put the razor down. His reflection held it up.

"They're right about the invasion," he heard his reflection say. "In fact, we're invading you right now." Then he reached out of the mirror and cut Jake's throat.

George Nikolopoulos is a speculative fiction writer from Athens, Greece, and a member of Codex Writers' Group. His short stories have been published in over 60 magazines and anthologies including Galaxy's Edge, Nature, Daily Science Fiction, Factor Four, Grievous Angel, Best Vegan SFF, and The Year's Best Military & Adventure SF.
Website: georgenikolopoulos.wordpress.com
Twitter: @g_nikolop

No Monsters
by Charlotte O'Farrell

My daughter pulled the covers around her head for protection, her eyes wide with fear.

"There's a monster in the wardrobe, Mummy!" she insisted.

Smiling, I went over and pretended to check it out.

A scaly claw extended from the darkness, grabbing me by the throat and pulling me in. In the dark dungeon within, I saw the last three owners of the house, emaciated and cowering. Shackles like theirs shot out of nowhere and fastened themselves around my neck, arms and legs.

"See, darling? No monsters!" said a voice that sounded like mine, closing the wardrobe door behind me.

Charlotte O'Farrell is a lifelong horror fan who writes about all manner of the weird and wonderful. Her work can be found at the Drabble, the Rock N Roll Horror Zine and Horror Tree, among other places.
Twitter: @ChaOFarrell

Cold
by Andreas Hort

She pushed until her stomach felt like it was about to explode. She felt the baby slide out of her. She was drenched in cold sweat, exhausted, panting—but relief washed over her nevertheless, and she smiled lightly.

"I want to see him," she said in a weak, quivering voice.

"I'm cold!" yelled a high-pitched voice.

An ominous sensation crept up her back. She felt something spreading her. She looked down. A red, wrinkled baby face glared at her from between her thighs.

"I'm cold!" it screamed before shoving its head back into her.

She shrieked as it crawled in.

Andreas Hort resides in a small town in the northern part of the Czech Republic. When he is not earning his daily bread working various, usually physically oriented jobs, he writes and takes steps toward his goal to move to an English-speaking country. He was never published in English before. In his free time, he works out, studies the investment business, and, of course, reads.
Facebook: andreas.hort.71
Twitter: @Ondrej_Hort

Phases
by Michael Balletti

The crescent moon glowed like a silver canoe in the night sky, taunting the solitary figure who stared up from a deserted street corner.

Had it only been a week since the transformation?

A slight smile cracked the man's stern countenance as he recalled the bittersweet memory. The change had been agonising, of course, but the reward so satisfying. And the chase was better than the catch.

But that flickering smile died as soon as he realized his cruel predicament. It was torture, he mumbled angrily to himself, giving a man wings and then telling him when he could fly.

Michael Balletti lives in New Jersey. His work has appeared in Drabbledark: An Anthology of Dark Drabbles, Nothing's Sacred: Vol. 4, Scifaikuest, Theme of Absence and 200 CCs, among others.

The Prince
by Martin Eastland

The blood ran down his face, his petrified eyes scouring mine for mercy but finding none. He had dared to avenge his younger brother, himself foolish enough to defy my father. That would be impermissible. Subjugation of one's subjects is crucial in maintaining order, or anarchy will reign until it is met with equal resistance. These words of my father I remembered, staring vacantly into that devil Turk's dark eyes, moments only before I ripped them from his head. It would be dinner soon. I left two guards and returned to my quarters, eager to please her before the banquet.

*Born in Glasgow, Scotland, **Martin Eastland** began his writing career at the age of 12, his only outlet allowing him to escape a less than harmonious childhood. Almost 30 years later, he has gone from strength to strength as a writer, expanding into new areas, but remaining loyal to his preferred genres of horror, and the suspense-thriller. He enjoys mainly short stories and flash fiction as he views it as being beneficial for his future development as an author. He is happily married with four children, and lives with his wife in Shropshire, England.*
Facebook: Martin-Eastland-245154596385827

Dragon's Truth
by Crystal L. Kirkham

His orders were to destroy the dragon, but it seemed a pity to kill this majestic beast. He threw his spear and failed. Flames rushed past, missing him easily. A thought occurred to the knight. "Did you miss on purpose?"

The dragon hesitated. "Yes."

"Aren't you the one killing the people?"

"It's the princess," the dragon growled, "She's a shapeshifter."

He heard truth in the dragon's words. He'd sworn his allegiance but, he cared more for the people than dishonest royals. He considered the options: to do what's right or ignore his oath?

"I'll help you before she kills again."

Crystal L. Kirkham resides in a small hamlet west of Red Deer, Alberta. She's an avid outdoors person, unrepentant coffee addict, part-time foodie, servant to a wonderful feline, and companion to two delightfully hilarious canines. She will neither confirm nor deny the rumours regarding the heart in a jar on her desk and the bottle of reader's tears right next to it. Her paranormal urban fantasy series, Saints and Sinners, is available on Amazon and her YA Fantasy, Feathers and Fae will be released October 11, 2019, from Kyanite Publishing.
Website: www.crystallkirkham.com

The Shear-Thing
by Graham Robert Scott

Shear-Thing is an assemblage of old farm tools. Shears, hooks, scythes. A circular saw with chipped teeth. A rusting machete.

It moves, despite metal parts, with the pillowy sound of grain in breeze.

And it smells fear.

What happens is this: Someone makes you run. Someone makes you scared. As your monster reaches for you, Shear-Thing reaches into him, wiggling rusty blades through spongy lungs. Drags him gurgling into the dark.

The bodies are planted in the yard of the chief of police, who doesn't much care what real monsters do, until one day a gardener mows over some fingers.

Graham Robert Scott writes tales that are wry, dark, and speculative. He's published science-fiction in Nature, horror in Barrelhouse Online, and really tiny stories in 50-Word Stories and on his Twitter feed. His personal website takes its name from the prehistoric bear-dog, a toothy hunter that (like the platypus) couldn't quite make up its mind what it was. As a college professor by day and creative writer by night, Graham identifies.
Website: hemicyon.wordpress.com
Twitter: @graythebruce

Under the Bed
by G. Allen Wilbanks

"No more games. Go to sleep," the boy's father growled.

An angry slap at the wall switch plummeted the room into darkness and his father disappeared into the hallway.

The child watched in growing dread as his bedroom door clicked shut, closing out any remaining hope of salvation. He burrowed helplessly into his pillow, curling up into a tight ball to make himself as small as possible. He sniffled, then wiped at his cheeks with an already damp pajama sleeve.

"Yes, small thing," came the low, hissing voice once again from under the bed. "No more games. Go to sleep."

G. Allen Wilbanks is a member of the Horror Writers Association (HWA) and has published over 50 short stories in various magazines and on-line venues. He is the author of two short story collections, and the novel, When Darkness Comes.
Website: www.gallenwilbanks.com
Blog: DeepDarkThoughts.com

Swallow
by J. Rohr

Floating in the Pacific, I didn't know anywhere could be so peaceful. Years as a corporate hatchet erased such memories. A colleague's route to more layoffs took me by a beach. Sirens sang. I soon waded in wearing my suit.

Eventually, gargantuan teeth filled the sky. The behemoth's mouth closed. In darkness I tumbled, battered backwards by a tremendous tongue. The space tightened. Down a slippery throat I plunged, choking on leviathan's saliva.

The oesophagus opened suddenly, dropping me into a meaty vat of acid. Reflexively gasping filled my lungs with burning juices. Melting, I almost laughed. This felt right.

J. Rohr is a Chicago native with a taste for history, and wandering the city at odd hours. He writes a blog and has the band Beerfinger in order to deal with the more corrosive aspects of everyday life.
Website: www.honestyisnotcontagious.com
Twitter: @JackBlankHSH

Ribbit
by J.D. Bell

Sheriff Holiday bent down to examine the shoreline near the chemical plant. The water held tints of orange and reeked of rotten eggs.

As he stood, he spied a frog with red and yellow eyes and a head the size of a large dog watching him. The frog's throat ballooned out as the critter released a loud, bellowing croak. Its enormous mouth opened to expose rows of jagged teeth. The creature's tongue shot out and grabbed the sheriff around the throat, pulling him in like a tasty fly. Muffled cries faded as the croaking of mutant frogs filled the night.

J.D. Bell is an award-winning, internationally published, author of flash fiction and short stories. He recently retired from the world of writing advertising copy and is now enjoying the universe of creative fiction.
Facebook: jim.writes.stories
Twitter: @JimBell58

Water Leaper
by Raven Corinn Carluk

Splat.

The young couple stopped kissing to look for the source of the noise. Julia spotted it first. "Ewww. What is it?"

What appeared to be an ugly toad had jumped into the boat. Roughly the size of a grapefruit, it had mottled black skin with lime green eyes. It blinked, shifted, revealing that it wasn't a toad.

The little beast had wings instead of arms, and an arching scorpion tail. It hopped without hind legs, bouncing closer to them.

Trevor jumped up and stomped on it, then scraped the mess off his shoe. "All better. Where were we?"

SPLAT!

Raven Corinn Carluk *is an indie author of dark fantasy and paranormal romance.*
Website: RavenCorinnCarluk.Blogspot.Com

A Different Kind of Monster
by E.L. Giles

Monsters don't always have fangs and claws, nor do they suck your blood. They aren't always the materialisation of the nightmares that keep us awake all night long.

Sometimes, monsters bear a familiar smile and hold your hand when you're frightened as the night grows too dark. And it's then, when the lights are off, that the monster in them awakens.

Monsters don't always have fangs and claws, nor do they suck your blood. But they do lurk in the darkest spots of the night, predators and soul eaters, consuming your very essence before the lights are turned back on.

E.L. Giles is a dreamer, passionate about art, a restless worker and a bit of a weird human. He started his artistic journey as a music composer until the need to put his thoughts and stories down on paper grew too strong for him to resist it any longer. He lives in the French Province of Quebec, Canada, with his girlfriend and two boys.
Facebook: elgilesauthor
Website: www.elgilesauthor.com

Good Genes
by Alexander Pyles

I did not want to be chosen. Yet, when they came, I went with them. There were phrases like "your genes are excellent" and "you are needed," but I had no idea what any of that meant.

After a couple of weeks of being shuffled between laboratories and holding rooms, testing this and that, was I brought to an oppressively vast chamber.

Chains were affixed to my wrists and ankles. A haze clouded my resistance. A single word was scratched into the floor: EXALTED.

A rush of hot breath filled the chamber, warming my prickling skin. The maw enveloped me.

Alexander Pyles resides in IL with his wife and children. He holds an MA in Philosophy and an MFA in Writing Popular Fiction. His short story chapbook titled, "Milo (01001101 01101001 01101100 01101111)," from Radix Media, is due out fall 2019. His other short fiction has appeared on 101fiction.org, River and South Review, and other venues. Website: www.pylesofbooks.com Twitter: @Pylesofbooks

The Power of Imagination
by R.J. Meldrum

The character in his new story needed to summon a demon. The incantation had to look authentic. He closed his eyes and opened his mind. Words flowed. He scribbled them down as they entered his mind. He read what he had written. It was gibberish, a potpourri of nonsense words and phrases. He whispered them, to make sure the text flowed. There was a flash of light. In front of him stood an inhuman monstrosity. Red, black and covered in flames. The demon gazed at him.

"Thanks human. I don't know how you did it, but you opened the gate."

R. J. Meldrum is an author and academic. Born in Scotland, he moved to Ontario, Canada in 2010. He has had stories published by Horrified Press, the Infernal Clock, Trembling with Fear, Darkhouse Books, Smoking Pen Press, and James Ward Kirk Fiction. He also has had stories published in The Sirens Call e-zine, the Horror Zine and Drabblez Magazine. He is an Affiliate Member of the Horror Writers Association.
Twitter: @RichardJMeldru1
Facebook: richard.meldrum.79

Forbidden Love
by Henry Herz

"But, harsh! What dread through yonder window lurches?

It is the night, and foul Juliet a zombie.

Arise, black clouds, and kill the envious moon,

Who is already sick and pale with grief,

That thou her maid art far more horrifying than she:

She moans yet she says nothing: what of that?

Her eye falls out; I shall cherish it."

"Mmmm. Brains!"

"She speaks!"

"O Romeo, vampire! Wherefore art thou Romeo?

Deny thy raging bloodlust and refuse thy nature;

Or, if thou wilt not, bite deep my neck and be sworn my master,

And I'll no longer be a zombie."

Henry Herz edited the dark fantasy anthology, BEYOND THE PALE, featuring stories by Saladin Ahmed, Peter Beagle, Heather Brewer, Jim Butcher, Rachel Caine, Kami Garcia, Nancy Holder, and Jane Yolen. His horror story, Gluttony, will appear in the anthology, CLASSICS REMIXED. He authored the children's books: MONSTER GOOSE NURSERY RHYMES, WHEN YOU GIVE AN IMP A PENNY, MABEL & THE QUEEN OF DREAMS, LITTLE RED CUTTLEFISH, CAP'N REX & HIS CLEVER CREW, HOW THE SQUID GOT TWO LONG ARMS, ALICE'S MAGIC GARDEN, GOOD EGG AND BAD APPLE, TWO PIRATES + ONE ROBOT, THE MAGIC SPATULA, and I AM SMOKE.
Website: www.henryherz.com

Mirror, Mirror
by Stephen Herczeg

Sophie burst into the bathroom. She was running late, again. The bus would leave in ten minutes, if she missed it her boss would blow up, yet again.

She brushed her teeth, only one minute instead of the habitual two.

Cleanse, tone, foundation, blush, lipstick.

As she applied her eyeliner, she saw movement in her reflection. Something dark.

She turned, but the bathroom was an empty white void.

"Stupid idiot. Get moving," she cursed herself.

She turned back. The mirror was filled with teeth, claws, black fur and red eyes.

Sophie managed a short scream before the claws grabbed her.

Stephen Herczeg is an IT Geek based in Canberra Australia. He has been writing for over twenty years and has completed a couple of dodgy novels, sixteen feature length screenplays and numerous short stories and scripts. His horror work has featured in Sproutlings, Hells Bells, Below the Stairs, Trickster's Treats #1 and #2, Shades of Santa, Behind the Mask, Beyond the Infinite; The Body Horror Book, Anemone Enemy, Petrified Punks and Beginnings. He has also had numerous Sherlock Holmes stories published through the Belanger Books - Sherlock Holmes anthologies.

Social Media Zombie
by Rowanne S. Carberry

Blood drips from my mouth as I rip my dad's skull apart and claw at his brain. I know it's the only thing that will stop the hunger.

Looking back, I see my mum is still passed out in the hallway, the shock of seeing me too much for her after burying me.

I shovel more brain into my mouth, then sit back against the wall, stomach full. There's blood stuck under my broken nails and my mouth is covered in blood and brain.

That doesn't stop me snapping a picture. Uploading it online, I wait for the reaction.

#ImBackBitches

Rowanne S. Carberry was born in England in 1990, where she stills lives now with her cat Wolverine. Rowanne has always loved writing, and her first poem was published at the age of 15, but her ambition has always been to help people. Rowanne studied at the University of Sunderland where she completed combined honours of Psychology with Drama. Rowanne writes to offer others an escape. Although Rowanne writes in varied genres each story or poem she writes will often have a darkness to it, which helped coin her brand, Poisoned Quill Writing – Wicked words from a poisoned quill.
Facebook: PoisonedQuillWriting
Instagram: @poisoned_quill_writing

Reversing the Apocalypse
by Lydia F. Black

Backing up, she felt the cool texture of the brick building. *Cornered.* She'd have five, maybe ten seconds, if she wounded the zombie.

It limped closer, reaching out its bony hand.

She raised her gun, attempting to chamber a bullet. None fell into the barrel. *Shit.*

She knew the zombie—Dave—he worked at the restaurant downtown.

What if—?

Sighing, she seized the un-dead life-form and bit its shoulder.

Moaning, the zombie fell to the ground—its decaying flesh, smelling and tasting like rotten fish—and returned to its normal, pinkish state.

Dave looked up at his saviour, "What happened?"

*When she's not training for her third degree black belt, or slaving over the final days of school, **Lydia F. Black**, a ninja in Maryland, finds herself writing Drabbles, school papers, or the weird scenes in her head.*

ACKNOWLEDGEMENTS

We had another amazing number of submissions to this, the third in our DARK DRABBLES series of anthologies. There's such a lot of talented creativity in our universe, and everyone who sent us a terrifying teeny tale should be proud of their accomplishments.

We want to thank all the authors who support our crazy anthologies; without you, none of this would happen.

Thank you to the readers who continue to love this format. Please keep reading, we do it all for you.

To the people who surround us, help us, motivate us and listen to our wails; we love you.

www.blackharepress.com

Stories of new worlds, new creatures, alien colonisation, humanity's new home, space accidents, alien snackcidents, evil planets, military mashups, alien autopsies, and much, much more.

Beatific angels, holy wars, kitty saviours, epic battles between good and evil, devils and demons, fallen angels and many more tantalising tiny tales.

Wendigos, vampires, things that go bump in the night or hide under the bed, witches, demons, upirs, kelpies, toad people, zombies, sirens and hundreds of other tiny terrifying tales.

Micro myths of the paranormal;
poltergeists, spirit boards, ghosts
and ghouls, avenging apparitions
and horrifying hauntings.

Murder mysteries, criminal chronicles, whodunnits, revenge, suspicion, mayhem, intrigue, and lots more.

* 9 7 8 1 9 2 5 8 0 9 1 8 3 *